THE
LADY
with the
PURPLE HAT

THE
LADY
with the
PURPLE HAT

—— A NOVEL ——

OTILIA GRECO

THE LADY WITH THE PURPLE HAT
A NOVEL

iUniverse books may be ordered through booksellers or by contacting:

iUniverse
1663 Liberty Drive
Bloomington, IN 47403
www.iuniverse.com
1-800-Authors (1-800-288-4677)

ISBN: 978-1-5320-1319-5 (sc)
ISBN: 978-1-5320-1321-8 (hc)
ISBN: 978-1-5320-1320-1 (e)

Library of Congress Control Number: 2017901725

Print information available on the last page.

iUniverse rev. date: 3/29/2017

ABOUT THE BOOK

The Lady with the Purple Hat puts readers at the edge of their seats from the very beginning.

Daisy is the lady in the purple hat, and we are immediately engaged with Daisy in her insane strategy to not be recognized by wearing an outlandish, garish purple hat as she swans through the hospital corridors hell-bent in her resolve to enter her dying husband's hospital room to speed his death by poisoning him. Who is the crazed woman in the purple hat? We readers must know why she is doing this and what the backstory behind this evil act is that introduces the main character in the novel.

The reader must now find the answers to the question of who Daisy is and how she became the lady in the purple hat in this Hitchcock thriller opening scene. It is virtually impossible for the reader to put the book down. The story of Daisy is compelling and unique in it being the tale of how an innocent, young Daisy grows to become the person we see at the introduction of the story. This dark tale changes from its gothic tone and lifts toward the ending, giving light and renewed faith in the human spirit with its surprising ending.   V. Schiro

Also by Otilia Greco

Dreams: An Odyssey of Love and Mystery
Angelica's Discoveries: Romance and Journey to the New World

Pacific Book Review

Author Otilia Greco's novel, Angelica's *Discoveries: Romance and Journey to the New World* is a moving tale of discovery; an adventure about a brave woman's journey to find herself.

Angelica is a woman living in the Swiss Alps during World War II. While her father prefers her to stay home, she wants to travel to America and visit her beloved Uncle Victor. She leaves Switzerland to become a tourist's guide in Greece. While traveling, she ultimately falls in love and marries. When her husband Mark leaves Europe for America, Angelica leaves behind everything she knows to travel to accompany him, finally seeing her Uncle Victor and creating a new life.

Angelica's Discoveries is a charming and uplifting novel. Angelica is a courageous character that fights her fears with a tenacity that's admirable. From facing her small fear of water by sailing on boats to her larger fear of defying her father by moving overseas to the United States, she is a true hero in this novel. The romantic elements of *Angelica's Discoveries* are also a touching part of the story. Angelica's relationship with Mark throughout their trek across America is a testament to true love.

Greco's writing captures the full dimensions of the characters. Her vivid descriptions of Europe and America during World War II will transport readers back in time. Greco grew up in the Swiss Alps and describes the beautiful scenery with an unparalleled first hand recollection in this novel. The descriptions of the boats across Europe showcase the dangers of travelling at the time. Greco's writing about Angelica and Mark's adjustment to life in America captures the arduous journey immigrants experienced once they reached their adopted homes.

Angelica's Discoveries would be a great choice for readers who want a novel about a light romance with an inspirational message. *Angelica's Discoveries* will especially inspire female readers of romance or historical romance novels with her strong female protagonist. This story would also be an excellent choice for those who like historical fiction like Diana Gabaldon's *Outlander*, or books about immigrants in America such as Willa Cather's *My Antonia*. This book will also appeal to book clubs and readers that are looking to discuss new novels that explore complex issues such as immigration in a simple, relatable way.

Angelica's Discoveries is an empowering story that is short, but will leave a long impression on readers.

For Mr. Vic

PART 1

1

Without the slightest noise, Daisy turned the handle and slowly opened the door of hospital room 744. A large purple hat covered most of her pale face. She peeked into the patient's room.

Is he still alive? she thought.

Shouldn't he be dead by now?

Daisy wondered how much longer it might take until his last breath finally extinguished his life. He had to die soon.

In her elegant black designer purse, she carried a small perfume bottle filled with poison. Her heart was full of anger, and she was ready to take any risk. This chance had to be taken now.

Their divorce procedure was almost through; it had taken more than ten years. So many things had to be resolved by the perseverant lawyers first.

Some days ago, Daisy bought this large purple hat, purple like the leaves of the mini Japanese red maple tree called bloodgood. Daisy never wore large hats. On the rare occasion she did wear a hat, it would be small and distinguished dark blue or black, never one of such a striking color.

However, today she planned to impress, blur, or shock. She'd selected this large purple hat to attract every observer to it rather than to her face. She chose to simply hide and not be recognized, pretending to be somebody else. She was fully loaded with hate. In fact, she was driven by hate and was prepared to perform like an actress onstage.

2

Daisy was an elegantly dressed woman in her early fifties. She was slim and attractive, with icy-blue eyes, short black hair, and a permanent Mona Lisa smile. Daisy had always been the kind of person asking for lots of attention; everybody around her had to fulfill her desires according to her wishes. She was an extremely demanding woman surrounded by lots of material goods: luxurious jewelry, expensive clothing, shoes that always matched her handbags. She liked to show off constantly and impress everyone in such a way that people immediately saw she was rich and powerful. If Daisy did not get what she wanted, she knew how to put on the pressure; her greed had to be satisfied.

In addition to the divorce proceedings dragging on for years, now her husband had become deathly ill, and she therefore wanted to discontinue the divorce and instead be his widow. Being a widow would position her in a much better light in high society. Her reputation would be more respectable. She also calculated that as his widow, her legal rights would mean inheriting a lot more than she would get from their divorce judgment. Furthermore, her lawyers were still uncertain as to how much money they could force him to pay. She figured that at her husband's funeral, her tears would impress his friends and their neighbors. Everybody would sympathize with her theatrical pain. All these reasons motivated her to buy the purple hat and hatch this crazy plan: Bernard had to die before the divorce was final.

Her first task was finding out how serious his illness was.

She discovered that her husband didn't have long to live. By the judge's ruling, the divorce was scheduled for the end of the next month.

Bernard had to die … and soon.

It was in late spring over ten years ago that Daisy left her husband and found a decent apartment in a typical English redbrick building at the outskirts of the city, in a romantic area near a small creek. However, she was not too happy in that neighborhood. Daisy had the feeling the neighbors checked on her and her doings. Usually Daisy took a walk around her block every morning.

She didn't want anyone to see her driving her car away from the apartment this Tuesday morning, April 7, so she decided to walk for more than twenty minutes along the small creek, then cross several busy roads to reach the hospital where her husband, Bernard, was lying, as she had secretly found out.

After crossing the small wooden bridge, she felt her anticipation grow. She could actually hear her heartbeat and her breathing increase. For a few minutes, she stopped to watch some ducks swim in the creek. Although she was observing the beauty of this quietness, she was unable to enjoy it. Today this idyllic atmosphere rather irritated her. Walking through the heavy morning traffic and crossing several noisy streets with the smell of gasoline enhanced her will to execute her plan at any risk!

A recent special court order determined that Daisy had lost her right for any contact with Bernard. The hospital management enforced this order strictly. However, Daisy was sure she had found a way to bypass the court order today.

4

When she arrived at the hospital entrance, Daisy pulled her large purple hat low down on her face and bent her head slightly downward. Today she was wearing a dark gray business suit with a white blouse and a light gray scarf in order to look formal and businesslike. She was convinced that nobody could recognize her in this outfit. She had to impress the hospital reception by acting like an important business representative, and this disguise might empower her to bypass any screenings.

It was quite early; seven thirty Tuesday morning, far too early for the patients to expect visitors. When Daisy reached the hospital receptionist desk, a woman was busy explaining the daily activity plan to some employees. None of them noticed Daisy passing. Daisy felt relieved not to have to explain her arrival. She quickly continued toward the elevator, ready to enter. Inside the cabin, she pressed the button to the seventh floor. As the elevator gained height, floor by floor, her heart started pounding. Luckily, nobody entered the elevator as it climbed to the seventh floor.

Leaving the elevator, Daisy marked her determination by taking large marching steps along the endless and deserted hallway to reach Bernard's room, number 744.

5

During the last week, she had meticulously plotted every detail of this journey, starting by locating which hospital Bernard was actually in. After several phone calls pretending to be a social adviser, she had found out his room number. She then had to find out the most appropriate timing for her visit and decide how to dress. Her next task was to study how to act if someone asked her the purpose for her visit. Several times she rehearsed in front of her mirror how to act professionally, pretend to be on duty, and check on the nurses' performance.

Daisy was eager to see him die soon.

She had decided this fate for the man she once fell in love with, the man who tried to fulfill all her desires, the man who spoiled her until the day she became greedier and never stopped demanding.

6

Daisy was glad not to meet any nurse along the white hospital hallway loaded with the distinctive hospital odors. Nobody seemed to be around. All the nurses were probably busy washing and medicating their patients. The door of room 722 was open, the red light over the door blinking. Daisy heard the sounds of pots and a trolley of medications being pushed around. She stopped to wait until that door closed before continuing to her destination: room number 744.

She paused in front of hospital room 744, and suddenly an unforeseen possibility crossed Daisy's mind:

What if a nurse is in Bernard's room right now?

For a fraction of a minute, she hesitated to open the door. However, there was no red light blinking. She reasoned that the chance of a nurse being inside Bernard's room was slim. Daisy took a deep breath while preparing her thoughts about how to react if a nurse was inside. She would say, *"I have been sent by the hospital quality supervisor to see how this hospital deals with seriously ill patients."*

Depending on the nurse's reaction, Daisy was well aware that this excuse could be risky.

She made a quick check to be sure her hat was in the right

position, arranged her gray silk scarf, and gave herself a pep talk. After a deep breath, she carefully placed her ear to the door. Then she silently put both hands on the door handle, pressed it down quietly, and slowly pushed the heavy door open. There was neither a sound nor any movement from inside the room.

Bernard must be asleep, she thought.

The door opened toward the opposite wall of the patient's bed, and all she first saw was a bright white wall with a painting of a black racehorse. Near the wall was a small table holding a yellow tray with a pot of fresh tea and a cup ready to be served to the patient.

Daisy's hand slipped into her purse, checking for the small poison bottle. Checking on Bernard's position, she thought, *Damn it! Why does the bed have to be on the opposite side of the door?*

This required pushing the door fully open to see the patient. Giving a further push, she was able to peek around the heavy door to check on her husband. Holding the door handle with one hand and the door itself with the other hand, she leaned her head forward to observe the sleeping patient, who she now considered her enemy.

What an immense shock! It hit her like a poisoned arrow.

A woman was sitting quietly next to his bed.

The woman must have watched her the entire time.

Daisy guessed this might be Bernard's girlfriend, who was taking care of him during the night. Whoever this woman was, she could not know who Daisy was under the big purple hat.

Confronted with the unexpected situation, Daisy wanted the woman to think that she'd walked into the wrong patient's room. She immediately stepped back, closing the door and mumbling, "Excuse me. I missed the room."

What should I do now? she asked herself.

This unexpected encounter with the woman sitting next to

Bernard's bed paralyzed Daisy. She needed to ponder how to escape unseen out of this hospital.

Near the elevator entrance, two female nurses were discussing a medication for a patient. Fortunately, the two nurses did not spot Daisy standing around the corner. Daisy waited nervously until the nurses disappeared into another patient's room.

The door of room number 744 unexpectedly opened, and the woman who was sitting at Bernard's bed stood in front of her.

Calmly she said in a soft voice, "You must be his wife. You *are* aware of the court order that determined you are never allowed to visit him in this hospital."

Taken aback, Daisy answered in a frosty voice, "And you must be Bernard's mistress. Am I right?"

With no remark, the soft-voiced woman gently backed inside and closed the door.

No further comment was necessary. Daisy had been caught and needed to exit the hospital before any hospital authorities or nurses could have her arrested. Even worse, they might find the poison in her purse.

Where can I hide the poison? Is there a wastebasket in the elevator? No, I can't dispose of it there. Somebody could find it. I have to escape with it. I hope nobody searches my purse on the way out!

The brief encounter with the woman in Bernard's room dramatically changed Daisy's role from the hunter to the hunted. She needed to flee and disappear quickly.

Her large purple hat, which she had especially purchased for this visit, now suddenly turned into a heavy burden. It was totally useless and a big liability. This moment had reversed the intended function of the purple hat; instead of hiding her face, it betrayed her and now made her vulnerable.

Why on earth did I never consider such a possibility?
Now everybody will see my extravagant large hat.

Is there no way to hide it?

Daisy tried to fold the hat in her hands. Still, everyone might recognize her, and possibly she would be arrested at the reception desk. The hat was far too large to fit into her elegant black leather purse, and she had no other bag to store it away.

There is no choice but to hide it or dispose of it.

In a panic, she folded it as small as possible and tucked it under her left arm.

Daisy knew what the court had clearly decided; she had absolutely no rights to disturb Bernard's privacy. However, driven by her bitter hate, she felt unable to let him die in peace.

She was ready to poison him, no matter what risk she had to take. She was ready to do anything to shorten his last days. After her plan failed, only destiny could help her to see him dead before the divorce was finalized.

7

Daisy was trapped; her immediate concern was how to exit this hospital. Her panic grew every minute because she expected Bernard's mistress might call the reception desk and have her arrested. One thought after another raced through her mind:

Why did the two nurses take so much time before deciding to enter the next patient's room?

What if someone's already in the elevator when I board it?

Why did I not think of such obstacles?

Daisy desperately needed to escape the hospital. She ran toward the elevator just before it took off to the next floor. Fortunately, nobody was inside. Immediately she pressed the button for the ground floor. She was relieved when the elevator's heavy doors closed. Hopefully it would not stop on its way down.

What if I'm arrested at the ground floor and, even worse, my purse is searched?

Daisy was nearing a nervous breakdown. The elevator's mirror reflected her pale face. Was it the face of a criminal?

The seven-floor descent seemed endless. Her heart was beating even louder than it had on her way up.

Once the elevator reached the ground floor, Daisy felt dizzy.

She left the elevator staring straight at the main entrance door, not looking right or left, pressing her purse and the purple hat tightly under her left arm.

A young nurse who had clearly noticed her nervous behavior ran toward her, saying, "Do you need help, ma'am?"

Daisy tried to continue her way toward the entrance.

"You are terribly pale, and you're not walking straight. You certainly are not looking well. Would you like me to call the emergency doctor?" the nurse insisted, holding on to her right arm.

"No, thanks. I'm just late and in a terrible rush. Where can I find a taxi?" Daisy nervously answered.

The young nurse shot a puzzled look at Daisy's badly folded purple hat and said, "Wait, I'll lead you to the main entrance. Just around the corner is the taxi stand."

"Thanks, this is very kind of you." Daisy, seeing the nurse staring at her purple hat, continued, "I need to be at a wedding in less than half an hour, and my son held me up at the hospital for so long."

"But at this hour, there's no visiting time here," the confused nurse responded.

"Thanks. Let me run; I cannot be late. My son just wanted to see the gift I bought for his friend's wedding."

Daisy finally made it to the taxi and opened the car door, saying to the driver, "Please drive me as fast as possible downtown near the shopping center."

By this time, Daisy was exhausted, and her heart felt like bursting. Sitting in the car's backseat, she tried to recover from her escapade. She felt like a rabbit chased by ten hunters.

Was I not a hunter myself once?

However, this time I am in line with the front end of a gun …"

This thought went through her mind repeatedly …

At the shopping center, Daisy paid the driver and ran off without waiting for her change, going around the corner to find the next cab. She boarded the new taxi and asked the driver to bring her back to her apartment.

Daisy was worn out, angry, frightened, frustrated, and obsessed by her only thought:

Bernard has to die ... and soon.

8

In hospital room 744, Bernard realized that someone had entered his room, but he was unable to identify the person.

Delirious, he muttered, "Was it Daisy?"

Half-conscious, he reviewed his life.

Bernard's intelligence and easygoing character combined with hard work made him successful in pursuing an exceptional career. He was highly respected in his trade. Everyone admired Daisy for being his wife and being able to participate in high society.

One day Bernard found out that Daisy charmed one of his rich business friends who could offer her far more luxury.

Obviously, Daisy was attracted by his wealth rather than by the man's personality.

The moment he had caught her having an affair with his friend, Bernard was terribly hurt that she had lied about being unfaithful. Thereafter, she was the one who filed for their divorce immediately. At this point, Bernard's love for her faded away.

After battling with several lawyers over the past ten years, Bernard's grief ended in a serious illness. His death was foreseen. The divorce was scheduled to be finalized by the end of next month. His last wish was to survive until the day the divorce was declared.

Bernard's and Daisy's lives started so differently.

9

Bernard was a good-looking young man, tall and bright, with blond, curly hair and hazel eyes. He intended to become a medical doctor. During his first year at the university, World War II started and Mother England called their young men for military service to defend their country against the Nazis. Because of Bernard's leadership skills and his performance, he was soon promoted from the position of a soldier all the way up to a lieutenant. Bernard hated the war, yet there was no alternative but to serve for several years.

One day the enemy forces caught him and several of his comrades. They were deported to a concentration camp at the very east border of Poland to Russia, where he was detained for many months near the end of the war. He and his comrades suffered from cold and hunger. They were forced to work hard in the fields, even in winter under icy weather conditions, when no farmer would work his land. Bernard and two other prisoners got ill, so the camp's sergeant shifted their tasks to the kitchen preparing soup, cutting bread, and cleaning the floors. At least it was not as cold as being outdoors during the damp, cold winter days.

The camp was an agglomeration of old wooden shacks, where the icy wind penetrated under the door and along the glass windows. The only warm room was the kitchen, heated by the wood fire of an old cooking stove. Each morning it took quite a while to initiate a new fire using humid wood logs and getting them to finally burn. Food was scarce and consisted mostly of a watery soup with few vegetables and some pieces of old bread. The good part was that the soup was warm. Each prisoner was glad to receive a bowl of warm soup, even if it often tasted sour or bitter, depending on the types of vegetables added.

During the cold winter days, the water pipe froze and water had to be carried in small buckets over a mile to the military kitchen. The nasty sergeant pushed the prisoners, commanding, "You must dig a trench all along the snow-covered fields from our shack to the distant water supply pipe; otherwise, I will find ways to poison you."

It took weeks to dig a trench for the pipe through the frozen ground until they reached the next water supply pipe. This job turned out to be extreme torture. Some prisoners' hands turned blue and were covered with blisters. One prisoner even lost one ear from frostbite. There was no choice. They had to obey.

One day the same camp's sergeant said, "Bernard, you are a clever young man. I can offer you a much better life. You just have to fight for us Nazis against our enemy. Will you accept this generous offer?"

"No, sergeant, I cannot fight against my own brothers," Bernard replied.

"Okay, I will give you one week to decide. The alternative is to be executed."

The camp managing sergeant was tall, choppy, tough, and harsh. He liked food, and whenever he could gather more soup than his soldiers received, with great pleasure he enjoyed eating it in front of them.

Bernard worked in the military kitchen. Occasionally

Bernard was able to prepare a better soup by adding certain spices or anything he could collect from an old farmer nearby. This changed the sergeant's mind, and he kept Bernard in the kitchen to continue feeding him richer food.

When preparing the daily bread provisions for each prisoner, Bernard began cutting slightly thinner slices. So he got a spare slice of bread to add to the sergeant's soup bowl and make his soup thicker.

One day by chance, one of Bernard's comrades found an old violin and a broken radio under a pile of garbage in a remote shack. What an exciting discovery for Bernard and his friends!

By stripping the strings from the old violin, one of his buddies, a technician, worked hard to connect one string as an antenna to the old radio battery, providing it with power. Now they were able to listen to the news from abroad. Obviously listening to any foreign radio station was totally forbidden. In total secret, they learned about the real war situation throughout Europe. Luckily, none of the guards ever found their hidden spot with the forbidden radio hidden under a stinky garbage pile.

Meanwhile Bernard's health grew worse and worse, and he became seriously sick with pneumonia. Instead of curing him, they forced him to retreat with the entire army all the way from the eastern end of Poland to Germany. Luckily, an English military troop liberated him and two of his friends.

Some weeks later, Bernard was able to find his way back home to England. It was only then that he realized his parents had passed away.

His local medical doctor was extremely concerned by his delicate health: Bernard had lost forty pounds, his cheeks were pale, and his brown eyes had lost their vivid look. The doctor hospitalized Bernard right away. It turned out he had contracted tuberculosis from undernourishment and wet lodging.

One year after the war was over, in 1946, the doctor sent him to a Swiss mountain village for a two-year recovery period to cure his illness. It was well known that the germs do not survive in high altitude. Thus this was a safe and promising cure against the disease.

10

During the war and shortly thereafter, almost no foreigners visited Switzerland or the High Alps. In the small mountain village, the schoolchildren were attracted by anybody speaking a foreign language. Because of Bernard's heavy accent, they nicknamed him "the Foreigner."

Captured as a prisoner of war, he had picked up words and expressions in Polish and had learned the German language. With this training, it was not overly difficult for him to pick up the local Swiss German dialect rapidly.

Bernard adapted fast to the lifestyle of this small village set in a beautiful landscape with snow-white mountain peaks and glaciers. A river divided green meadows where cows and goats were grazed. Most locals were friendly farmers. They helped him out with warm clothing. In return, he gave English lessons to their children.

A few years after the war was over, the English and other European tourists started to return to the nearby resort to spend their vacations in the clean mountain air.

As the days and months passed, Bernard's strength slowly recovered, and he decided to search for an occupation. Bernard was happy to find a job at the local doctor's office.

The doctor needed a translator for explaining treatment and medication to the British tourists.

At the doctor's office, Bernard met Anthony, who was the doctor's assistant. Anthony and Bernard became good friends. One evening Anthony invited his new friend for dinner at his parents' home. Anthony's grandmother had been English, so his mother still spoke Bernard's language fluently. Anthony's family was open-minded and often invited "the Foreigner" to their home. Bernard was delighted to find a new family at Anthony's house. Anthony and Bernard remained lifelong friends.

Bernard had spent almost four years in the war, followed by two years of recovery in the Swiss mountains. Thereafter, Bernard was too old to continue his medical studies. Too many years had gone by since he was forced to leave the university in London. The war had blown away his career plan to become a medical doctor. During these years, he had lost both of his parents, and the family fortune was gone. Bernard's father fell under the enemy's weapons in Europe, and his factory was set on fire during the war. Bernard's mother died only days before the war was over. Possibly she died of grief, not knowing if Bernard, her only son, was still alive after he had been deported to Poland.

At age twenty-nine, Bernard had to make up his mind to find new ways to earn his living. He dreamt of starting his own business. Bernard was clever and had inherited his father's business-oriented mind.

One day Bernard met an English guest at the village doctor's studio. He was planning to export and distribute a new medication in Europe. The English chemist needed someone commanding several languages, and he approached Bernard:

"Bernard, you are fluent in English, German, and French. I am convinced that you are the right man to introduce my medication to other countries. Would you like to work for me?"

"Well, I am touched that you asked me. I am currently seriously considering a way to find a challenging job," Bernard answered.

The English guest was delighted to find an enthusiastic young man eager to work for him.

Bernard started to make contacts and worked intensively to achieve his goals to become the continental distributor. He had to travel quite a bit to develop his growing business.

However, he still lived in the Swiss mountain village that he now considered his home.

D aisy grew up as the only daughter of a grocery store owner in a small English country town. She was pretty, with an innocent face, ice-blue eyes, and black hair. Although kind, she wasn't known for being the most literate person. Daisy was practical and planned to be a salesperson at her father's store someday.

However, her life changed at nineteen, when she accepted an offer from a rich client of her father's to spend a vacation in the Swiss mountains with them. Her task was to look after their five small children while the parents went skiing. This was to be Daisy's first trip away from home and abroad.

In contrast to her family's simple way of life, Daisy was impressed by the wealth of the extravagant family. They flew first class to Switzerland. At the airport of Zurich, a limousine waited for the large family to drive them for several hours along some lakes, followed by an area with meadows where some cows were grazing. The driver served hard drinks to the couple and lemonade to the children and Daisy. Soon all five children fell asleep, and their parents and Daisy contemplated the changing of the landscape as they passed by some idyllic villages. They even saw ruins of old castles.

As soon as the limousine started to climb the narrow mountain pass road, they hit snow. After each bend, there was a higher wall of snow along the road border. Daisy was in awe. She had never seen so much snow in England. After many bends, they reached the top of the pass, and then the turns of the road brought them down toward the Engadin valley, enveloped by the most beautiful mountain ranges and totally covered by a soft cover of snow. The sun was shining, the sky was clear blue, and the snow twinkled. Daisy thought she was dreaming—the scene looked like a fairy tale.

Finally they reached their destination: one of the most expensive and noble hotels of the elegant mountain resort. The family occupied two suites, one for the couple and one with three bedrooms for the children and Daisy. Most meals for the children were served in their suite while the parents dined in an elegant dining room with many guests from all over the world.

Daisy was impressed by the wealth of many other guests residing in the Palace Hotel. Part of her job was looking after the children, bringing the older children to the ski school and taking the small children for walks on a sled or playing with them in the snow, building snowmen. She adored being around so many children and did an excellent job in occupying them day after day. The couple was happy to enjoy their vacations not having to take care of their children and being able to spend their time with the other guests at some glamorous parties.

Daisy decided never to sell vegetables at her father's store again; her dream was to work with children and become a kindergarten teacher.

During this time, Daisy developed her deep desire to become rich some day and to be able to buy whatever she wanted or dreamt of. There must be a way to become rich and avoid selling fruits and vegetables at her father's store all her life.

What about getting married to a son of a rich family?

She made up a plan to watch out for a suitable husband, a lawyer, a dentist, or a medical doctor, someone who earned lots of money.

The following year, she welcomed a second chance to return to the Swiss mountain resort with the same wealthy family and take care of their children. She entrenched her calculated dream even deeper.

However, destiny often plays another role than planned.

12

One day at a bar, Daisy got to know "the Foreigner," Bernard While. He was strolling through this opulent place with some local colleagues from a nearby village. She got his attention because he spoke her language. Could he be from England?

He was a good-looking young man. Daisy assumed that he must have rich parents to be able to spend his vacations at this expensive resort. So she decided to question him:

"Do you enjoy your vacations here? In which hotel are you residing?"

"I like this valley; however, I am not spending my vacations here. I've lived and worked in one of the nearby villages for over two years now. This is the first time I decided to stroll around and take a look at this elegant resort. By the way, what brings you here?"

"Well, I am taking care of some rich children while their parents are out skiing," Daisy answered.

"So you are working, too, and not just vacationing in such a snobbish place."

Bernard seemed relieved to see that Daisy was not an extravagant and spoiled young woman. That led to more conversation, and they decided to meet again soon. She was charmed and delighted about the handsome young man with curly, blond hair.

Even though Bernard did not fit exactly into her plan of landing a rich boyfriend, they soon fell in love.

Daisy watched over the family's children perfectly and earned quite a bit of money. Bernard was busy building up his new business, importing goods from England to Europe. It seemed a perfect match. She was charming and ready to help him in every regard. Bernard was delighted to have found his soul mate.

Since Daisy was in love with Bernard, she decided not to return to England with the English family. She remained in the Swiss mountain resort and was happy to accept an offer from an Italian family to take care of their two noisy children during their four weeks of vacation at the same hotel.

After the Italian guests left, Daisy continued working as a nanny and was employed by the hotel management permanently. She loved her job taking care of children while their parents took off for sports or amused themselves during the evenings.

13

Bernard's dwelling was a small studio in a house with locals. The village he lived in was only a few miles away from the elegant resort of St. Moritz.

Since Daisy started to work for the hotel, she was forced to stay at the hotel with the other employees. The quarters were simple, small, and rather dark, totally different from the elegant hotel room she occupied while caring for the children of rich families.

So Daisy decided to move in with Bernard.

His studio was not spacious, but at least it had a large window with a breathtaking view of the mountains. It was sunny and cozy; more importantly, it suited her better to be near her boyfriend.

However, neither Bernard nor Daisy had been aware how critically the locals took it that they lived together before being married. This fact contributed to the local gossip. Such behavior was not suitable and not acceptable in this small village.

Possibly, moral principles were different in England. However, in the small mountain village, this free lifestyle was not tolerated. Even so, Bernard persuaded his landlord that Daisy was his fiancée and that they planned to get married as soon as he had a steady income.

The local priest was shocked to learn of their arrangement. The priest was putting pressure everywhere. Villagers started to avoid Bernard and did not talk to him any longer. That pressure forced Bernard's landlord to expulse him from his studio. Even Bernard's doctor mentioned that he would be forced to lay him off and he would lose his job. It was simply not tolerated that the polite "Foreigner" behaved so immorally, even though he was well integrated into the village by now.

One day the priest personally stopped by Bernard's studio and forced Daisy to pack her stuff and return to the hotel's facilities until they were officially married.

In 1950, this was the mentality of a small mountain village where everyone knew everyone. Local moralities were strictly controlled by the priest, while the priest could not care less about the morals of the rich vacationers at the elegant resort just a few miles away.

14

One year later, Bernard and Daisy got married and decided to move back to England to Daisy's hometown near Bristol. Bernard worked his way up in the European distribution of pharmaceutical products. He was working hard and was proud of his success.

Back in England, Bernard had to drive to his new office for over three hours every day, which became tiring. Daisy had no real appreciation for her husband's efforts.

In the meantime, the couple had two sweet children, a boy named William and a girl named Nicole.

Some years later, Bernard wanted to move closer to town to have the convenience to take off by plane at any time for his expanding export business throughout Europe. Bernard found a lovely apartment for his family in the outskirts of London, right next to a park. All seemed to work out fine. However, Daisy did not like the apartment. She was not ready to leave her cozy English country house near the river. To Bernard's disappointment, Daisy said, "I'm not moving as I am seriously concerned the children would not like to grow up near the big city. Pollution might harm their health. I prefer to remain in my small town."

Two years later, Bernard came home with an offer of a

beautiful, huge villa situated near the woods at the outskirts of London, not far from his office. Still there was no way to persuade Daisy to move with the children.

In the meantime, Daisy had become a member of the local women's club, and of course she was highly admired by her former schoolmates because she had a husband who was earning more money than any other family in their small town. Daisy wore nice jewelry and expensive silk scarves to show off and impress her friends. In the summer, she was able to spend a month's vacation with their kids at the seaside.

Daisy was once the poor daughter of a simple grocery store owner, and she now enjoyed being special and envied by her peers. This was the main reason she was not keen to move to the city. She assumed that she possibly would meet many other rich women there.

"Here in my town, I feel like the princess; and in the city, I probably would not get the attention I want and enjoy. So we are not going to move," was her harsh response.

Bernard spoiled his wife because he felt bad leaving her with the children alone all day. Once he reached home at night, not much time was left to see or play with his children. However, he accepted this exhausting life to please his beloved young wife.

Eventually, Bernard persuaded Daisy to visit the city and join him at some business dinner parties. A maid was arranged to look after the children. Bernard was proud to introduce Daisy to his business friends. She was an attractive young woman, and of course she wore elegant, expensive dresses. She knew how to present her golden necklace on her pale décolletage. Daisy enjoyed being noticed; however, sometimes she felt embarrassed to be unable to join in on conversations about local politics or that she missed the points in high-level intellectual discussions. City people seemed more educated and more sophisticated in their selection of distinguished expressions and fine pronunciation. Daisy decided to attend courses on art history, politics, mineralogy, and jewelry. That way she was prepared to explain the special color of her emeralds to other women and show off with their value.

In her hometown near the River Thames, such education programs were not available, so she accepted driving with Bernard to the city one day per week. Her new schedule impressed the women from her local women's club. In the meantime, her kids were attending first grade and kindergarten. Daisy's maid took care of them while their mother was gone. Bernard decided to rent a nice townhouse apartment in the city so that Daisy had a place to relax and study in between her lessons at the university during the day. Soon Daisy needed a private teacher to adapt to the high-class pronunciation of her own mother tongue. She was eager to get that aristocratic touch.

The maid was taking good care of the spoiled children; they were well behaved and happy to finally have someone who had time to play with them. The elderly maid gave them much attention and love. She enjoyed often having them all to herself, slowly replacing their mother's love.

However, in her hometown, the fine language Daisy now spoke was received as a snobbish attitude, which the locals disliked. Soon her former schoolmates began to expulse her from local events. They did not appreciate her mentality and showing off, and they started to avoid her more and more.

Finally, the day came when Daisy decided to move to the city completely and get a large villa. The children insisted on taking along their maid, who had become their trusted surrogate mother. They loved her, and she loved them. A second, younger maid was employed for keeping the house clean and doing the cooking. Daisy decided the children needed to attend a private school. A personal driver was requested, as Daisy did not like to drive the busy city streets.

The villa had to be totally remodeled and furnished with the most expensive King Louis XV French antiques. Chairs needed to be recovered with an authentic white silk with beige velvet stripes. Silverware was needed, and the maid had to polish it daily. Expensive paintings that she collected at art auctions hung on the walls. Now Daisy was a lady … She finally managed to impress people in the city as much as she had hoped.

Daisy was happy adding a noble accent to her small talk and being able to impress friends with her newly acquired knowledge of art history. Her knowledge was not deeply rooted, so she was not aware that she frequently misinterpreted and mixed up some artist names and their work. Occasionally Bernard felt embarrassed, but not too many people seemed to notice Daisy's misinterpretations.

Bernard was happy to see her educate herself, but he never realized her growing pretentiousness. He was pleased to invite business people for dinner and show them his elegant, decorated home. The expenses of his wife's demands grew almost daily, and Bernard had to work even harder. Needless to say, Bernard was successful in his career, exporting the English medication to many countries throughout Europe. He was traveling a lot and intended to expand his business contacts to South Africa and later to North America.

D aisy was keen on spending her vacations in fancy places. The summer vacations on the English seashore did not have the warm water and the snobbish people she admired, as at the French Riviera. So Bernard rented a house on the French seaside, with a large deck looking onto the sea. Sometimes in the evenings, Daisy adored drinking one or two glasses of white wine while watching the sunset and impressing the passersby. The children enjoyed this vacation because they were able to fool around with the waves in the sea. Their younger maid was happy to spend the days with the children, bathing and playing with them instead of cleaning the house. In that climate and atmosphere, the children and the maid were full of energy and loved to play around the beach the whole day while Daisy met other wealthy women. Daisy decided to play bridge at the hotel terrace and enjoyed walking up and down the beach talking to elegant women. Here she was in her element, and she was sure to be noticed showing off with her highly fashionable bathing suits. Each day she selected a different color and style of suit. During the evening, she liked to mix with elegant people at the casino and gamble for money, always elegantly holding a glass of champagne in her left hand. She never admitted that in reality she hated drinking champagne.

However, she drank it because it looked good to do so, and this seemed to be the more important issue for her.

Bernard, as with most husbands, flew in to join his wife over the weekends only. Now he needed to meet the husbands of the women Daisy had spent most of the week with. Possibly one of the rich husbands could be helpful to Bernard's career, she concluded.

The Christmas holidays were spent in the Swiss Alps. It had to be in the world-famous winter resort, St. Moritz, the only place she felt to be adequate. She believed that this lifestyle might help Bernard meet even more important businessmen and add a lot to his reputation. Daisy loved to mix in this snobbish and elegant atmosphere. She walked around in her mink coat and designer dresses, and she adored being invited to parties and meeting people with even more wealth.

During one vacation at the elegant mountain resort, they were invited to the Richards' mansion. The husband was a rich manager of several companies. It was for a birthday party for his wife, Margot Richard. Mrs. Richard gave the guests a tour of her freshly remodeled mansion. Daisy was impressed by the large hallway, the entrance hall furnished with antique furniture, and the white marble floors covered with precious silk Persian rugs. Numerous large, antique Dutch paintings were hanging next to a beautiful Venetian mirror. The bathrooms shone with their golden faucets and Italian pinkish marble floors; a pleasant scent of bitter almonds gave the decor a special touch. Beautiful historical carved wooden panels decorated the bedrooms walls; the beds were fitted with pure silk bed linens and covered with real fox fur bedspreads. An elegant yellowish wall-to-wall carpet enhanced the large living room with white leather lounge chairs and a huge leather sofa, all the latest Italian style. The old clock overlooked the area from a corner and controlled the cozy atmosphere with hourly beats.

Meanwhile, in the dining room, an excellent dinner was served on a nicely decorated mirror table with lime-green candles reflecting in it. Elegant Danish silverware and white plates made the setting complete. Two male servants politely served a delicious meal, wearing dark blue coats with golden buttons and white gloves. Daisy was in awe by all this wealth combined with extremely good taste.

This event was the culmination of Daisy's vacation in St. Moritz. From then on, her dream was to remodel her home in London so it would be a similarly breathtaking mansion.

At midnight, all the guests got up and toasted with champagne the hour of Margot Richard's fiftieth birthday. The host raised his glass and gave a short speech to the guests, followed by remarkable words honoring his beloved wife. Then Mr. Richard explained that his surprise for Margot's birthday was in the garage. Everyone had to follow him there. There waited a brand-new shiny silver Maserati, of course one of the most expensive Italian luxury sport cars, especially tailored for Margot.

Delighted and surprised, Margot opened the garage door. Entering the car, she checked every single button and caressed the red leather seats with the fine smell of leather. After sitting in the car for a few minutes, she turned the key to start the engine. Carefully she stepped on the clutch and then shifted into the reverse gear. She prepared to slowly accelerate and back out through the open garage door. Suddenly, Margot's white pointed high heel shoe slipped off the clutch and she tried to stop the car immediately, yet she hit the accelerator and the car jumped with a dark roaring sound backward across the street and right into the opposite house wall.

All the guests jumped, frightened and screaming after that terrible moment. The accident shortened the car by nearly one yard. The brand-new beautiful car looked pitiful; all elegance was gone. The rear of the car had turned into a wreck of crashed metal.

Margot was clearly in complete shock. She was pale like a ghost, still holding on tightly to the steering wheel. She appeared to be unable to say a word or get out of the car. Huge tears, mixed with some blood from a small wound on her left cheek, ran along her face and onto her beautiful off-white evening dress.

Finally, her husband took a big breath and liberated Margot from her awful situation, helping her to force the car door open and climb out of the wreck. Shivering and crying in Mr. Richard's arms, Margot was inconsolable and more than embarrassed to find herself in this awful situation in front of all her guests.

Two men pushed the wreck slowly back into the garage and closed the garage door. Every invited person felt terribly sorry for Margot, and nobody knew what to say to end this long silence.

After Mr. Richard had composed himself, he said, "Dearest, luckily nobody is hurt. This is an accident, and you are not seriously wounded. It is only a matter of metal repair and paint. It doesn't matter. It's just a car. To celebrate your true birthday, I will order a new car for you tomorrow!

"Now, let's all go upstairs to recover and restart the party. You and all our guests need a brandy to calm down."

Everyone knew that Margot's husband was the kindest person, a gentle self-made man, always ready to help or please others. He liked his friends to participate in their wealth.

However, none of his friends ever realized that their hosts were rich but unhappy people. They had no children of their own. Mr. Richard was not healthy. He was systematically hiding away his terrible lung cancer. No one ever realized that some of his "extended business trips" actually consisted of surgery and special treatment therapies.

Daisy was not at all aware of the background troubles the Richards had. She only saw their wealth, and she was extremely impressed and envious of their lifestyle.

16

From that day on, she aimed to impress their friends in England the way the Richards did. She was determined to update and remodel their home in England with noble furniture and add many ultramodern gadgets to the interior, upgrading it to a similarly luxurious mansion. Daisy asked Margot for their Italian interior designer's address. Her plan was to fly him to England to advise Daisy how to turn her home into an eye-catching residence. The fox fur bedspreads and the shiny silk sheets in Margot's bedrooms had amazed her. She had already decided to order these items as soon as they were back in England. Daisy demanded a lot and aimed for even more.

Back home, she remodeled their bedroom with a brand-new king-size bed, electric blankets, and pink silk sheets. What a feeling to sleep in such luxury now! However, Bernard disliked the silk sheets because of the slippery feeling, and he hated the electric blankets because he'd overheat and have to move over to the bed's edge, where it was cooler.

One evening Bernard returned home overly tired from a long business trip with a delayed flight. Exhausted, he said, "Daisy, I don't feel so well. Possibly some fever has hit me."

Concerned, Daisy replied, "Go to bed, dear. I'll have some

tea made for you and bring you an aspirin, which should make you feel better."

However, during the night, his temperature raised immensely. Bernard was sweating and feeling seriously ill. An upset Daisy called the local doctor, who came in the middle of the night.

The doctor soon realized the cause of Bernard's illness.

"This bed is wired, my dear patient. It's not your body's temperature that is making you sweat. You are just exhausted, not seriously ill. It is that electric heated blanket switched to the highest temperature that puts you in this painful situation."

They all looked at each other and exploded in laughter. After removing the heated blanket, Bernard recovered quickly. Although Bernard had insisted that they remove the electric blanket on his side, the maid had changed the bed linens that morning and accidently placed Daisy's electric blanket on Bernard's side, invisible because it was hidden under another bed covering.

Bernard's business flourished, and he expanded his business activity to Germany, France, Italy, Belgium, and Sweden. He was traveling frequently, and several times he asked Daisy to join him on his trips to Paris, Florence, Venice, Brussels, and Stockholm.

They were able to buy a country home sitting next to the River Thames. A small wooden bridge connected the house with a small island where a historical out-of-order mill was located. It was a beautiful location; however, the house was rather run-down. Carpet covered only the first ten steps of the staircase; one could see the bare wood on the others.

Bernard was earning more money now, and Daisy was having an easy time spending Bernard's money by remodeling room after room in their new home.

Bernard was often invited to socialize with important and interesting executives and politicians. He believed this could have broadened Daisy's mind; however, Daisy accompanied Bernard only once. She found out that business traveling meant getting up early for boarding planes. She was also not keen on staying alone in her hotel room or walking around the streets in an unfamiliar town while Bernard was attending business meetings. Bernard's philosophy was to develop deep human relations, friendship, and camaraderie to help his partners out whenever needed. This was in total contrast to Daisy's superficial conversations and snobbish allures, which did not impress Bernard's friends. So she did not take any business trips with her husband again.

By working in different countries, Bernard had many interesting experiences, and he met a number of powerful men. On a trip to Sweden, he met Jack Barns, who was heading a large industrial company in addition to working for the country's politicians. After a successful introduction of Bernard's products, Jack became an outstanding, trusted, and close business partner and later a good friend.

One day Jack told Bernard, "I would love to invite you to spend two days at my hunting lodge situated in the north of Stockholm. Large woods surround the area, and for miles and miles, no other houses exist. That's where I escape from my hectic business life. You certainly will like the calm atmosphere there. It's a wonderful relaxing change from our busy business life. My friends will enjoy teaching you some hints for stalking animals and particularly hunting moose or elk."

Bernard accepted Jack's kind invitation and truly enjoyed the days with him and his hunting friends, the rural nature, and the outdoor life, even though he lacked the instincts of a hunter.

Back home, Bernard reported his special travel experiences.

18

Daisy was not paying attention, instead wanting to tell her husband about the silverware shopping she did while he was gone.

However, after Bernard told her about his hunting experience with Mr. Barns in Sweden, she was deeply impressed and decided right away to take some shooting lessons. Her desire was to be acknowledged as an extravagant woman who was still able to participate in exploring the wilderness and shooting big game.

While Bernard took off for another trip abroad, Daisy enrolled in shooting lessons at the local hunters club without letting Bernard know of her intent and new sport activities. She went downtown to find a special store that sold hunter clothing. She bought herself a complete stylish outfit: khaki-colored trousers, a matching T-shirt, and a greenish-gray windbreaker.

The teacher was plainly surprised to have a female student. He helped her rent a light 12-gauge shotgun. The shooting practice started with learning how to hold the gun firmly, place the elbows near the chest without any shaking or vibrations, keep the gun at a certain eye level, and focus on a white panel with a black center then slowly pulling the trigger to hit the center of the black dot. After becoming acquainted with the gun, she quickly achieved this goal. Days thereafter, her teacher had her shoot a clay pigeon placed on a wooden pole. After her fourth try, she hit the pigeon and it broke into a thousand pieces. Daisy was amazed by her success and loved the special moment of long-distance total destruction.

The next step was to learn to shoot a moving target. A cable on an electric winch pulled a piece of stuffed fur quickly along the ground, simulating a rabbit. Daisy even managed to hit this artificially moving rabbit. After eagerly taking every step to become a serious hunter, it was soon time to shoot real animals.

Her teacher was proud of her learning attitude, which was fed by a clearly determined mind. Some weeks later, the teacher took Daisy to the club's private hunting area. The next challenge was to hit wild pigeons. Daisy was excited and enjoyed being in the wilderness. Soon a wild pigeon was in sight. Daisy moved the gun up against her shoulder, held it firmly, and followed the pigeon by constantly aiming at it as it moved slowly along the grass.

The pigeon had to die.

The moment the pigeon took off from the ground, she pulled the trigger ... and hit it!

It fell dead not far from her feet, onto a pile of yellow and red leaves that had fallen from the trees since nature began to prepare for winter.

This excitement caused Daisy to feel her blood running faster through her veins. It was a mixed feeling of pleasure and achievement.

"I did it!" she happily exclaimed.

The next step was to pick up the dead bird and carry it over to her teacher, who was standing only ten yards behind her. He congratulated her and invited her to continue to hunt pigeons the next morning. Proud of her day's achievement, Daisy returned home.

*

As she recovered from the exciting day, sipping a cup of warm tea in her mansion, some strange thoughts went through her mind.

She suddenly remembered the day when she was a little girl, about seven years old, and she had found a wounded white pigeon in front of her family's front door. Slowly she approached the paralyzed bird with its broken wing. For a while, they both looked at each other with frightened eyes. The eyes of the bird seemed blurred and expressed its great pain. When she stretched out her little hand to pick up the bird, it just let it happen. Cautiously she took it in her small hands and carried it to her mother, who was ironing in their kitchen. Together they stuffed a cardboard box with a warm soft towel and laid the pigeon in it. Daisy began by feeding it water drops and later moved on to sunflower seeds. The bird became her patient and recovered slowly. She took good care of it daily, and one day the pigeon was able to walk around on their balcony. The pigeon became her pet and was quite tame. She named her pigeon Coco.

Soon Coco started to spread its wings and began to fly short turns, returning to land on her shoulder. Two months later, the bird did not return home …

Daisy could still feel her big disappointment today.

Her pet had left. She called its name, but it never showed up again. For many nights, the little girl prayed and wished that Coco would find its way back to her. Little Daisy often fell asleep with tears in her eyes. Why had her Coco disappeared?

At Christmas, her parents bought her a small stuffed white toy pigeon. For years and years, this stuffed pigeon sat on her light blue bedcover to welcome her home from school.

*

As she continued to reminisce, she realized that possibly a hunter had had an easy prey shooting her Coco.

Why did her pet have to die?

Daisy was in a dilemma. Today she'd hunted a pigeon!

As a child, she'd adored animals and now she was becoming a hunter. Her split feelings let her soon forget her childhood memories. She absolutely wanted to continue her snobbish lifestyle by being a hunting woman now. Thus the hunting lessons must continue. The next hunting exercise would be shooting wild rabbits.

Her husband, Bernard, had no idea about her hunting and its progress. She planned to surprise him with her talent at the appropriate moment. Her biggest desire was to be invited as a guest to Jack Barns's grounds and explore Sweden's wilderness.

19

Daisy insisted on coming along the next time Bernard was invited to participate in the men's passion. On this trip, she wanted to reveal to Bernard how well prepared she was for a hunting adventure.

Jack Barns was rich and owned a huge property with a well-equipped hunting lodge with several bedrooms and a dining room with a long table seating fourteen persons. Next door was the living room, with two dark blue sofas and matching chairs on a thick gray woolen carpet, well arranged and not too far from the fireplace.

Daisy was surprised to find Mr. Barns's hunting area far from any village or city. It was lost in solitude, surrounded by many huge trees. The cozy hunting lodge faced a small idyllic pond with ducks swimming on it. One could clearly smell the fresh odors of nature and hear many different birds singing.

While she was seated with Bernard, Jack, and three other men around the fireplace, Jack commented, "Tomorrow we'll go hunting. The target will be a big elk. We will split up in two groups and start at different ends of my property. Bernard and two men will form one group, and my brother and I will form the second group. Daisy, if you seriously want to participate, you are welcome to join my group."

"Yes, Mr. Barns, I absolutely want to join the hunting and am pleased to participate in your group. Who knows I might become a hunting addict," Daisy answered.

They excitedly began to make plans concerning how to proceed.

Early the next morning, at five o'clock, they started out after having a continental breakfast and a cup of strong coffee. All the hunters wore special greenish-gray outfits, rubber boots, and small green felt hats, which Jack had provided for everyone. Daisy had brought her own outfit. Jack supplied Daisy with a woman's gun. The two groups started walking ahead to their starting positions. It was quiet, and the grass was still covered with morning dew, a few drops falling from some low tree branches. The damp air lay over the fields before the sun started to rise and dry it with its warm shine. One could not hear the slightest sound as they moved silently along, hoping to track down the wild animal.

For two hours, no elk was spotted, not even any smaller dear.

The two groups then walked in radial directions so that the animals had no chance to escape a hunter's gun.

Daisy was the first person to spot the huge wanted elk; it was grazing under a small pine tree. She was holding her breath out of excitement. With the hunters' approach, the elk sensed the danger. It looked around, stretched his body, and started to run.

Daisy immediately brought her gun up in the right shooting position and pulled the trigger. *Bam!*

The elk abruptly pulled his head up, ran a few steps farther, tumbled, and fell dead on the grass. The elk had died!

All the hunters were visibly surprised by Daisy's fast reaction and her precise shot. Daisy enjoyed the men watching her shooting the large elk. They seemed somewhat shocked that she was able to react so fast and that the large elk fell to the ground right away. She was sure it was the first time any of them got to see an experienced and successful hunting woman in action.

The Swedish hunting tradition was that it was the hunter's job to place a branch of pine tree into the dead animal's mouth.

Jack Barns went to break off a branch of a nearby pine tree and handed it to Daisy, saying, "It is the hunter's honor to place a pine branch in the animal's mouth. After that, we need to take a picture of the successful hunter with the prey!"

For a second, Daisy hesitated to walk over near the dead elk. But she composed herself and proudly walked over to the prey.

She stood in front of the elk's head and had to bend over the dead animal to place the branch in its mouth. It was peacefully stretched out in the grass. She noticed the beautiful elk's horns and its well-shaped head.

Deep feelings of disgust and regret overwhelmed her suddenly: *She had been brutal; she had shot that majestic creature!*

Why did she allow herself to kill such an elegant living elk?

She was a mother of two lovely children. How could she ever explain this act to them? She decided never to hunt again.

For a split second, she had to conquer tears swelling up in her eyes. In the meantime, all the hunters surrounded her and expressed their excitement. They congratulated her warmly for a great achievement. Split between feelings of regret and great achievement, she ultimately rejected her reservations and convinced herself that hunting was a sport and she had made it.

Still, Daisy was pale.

Jack seemed to sense what was going on in Daisy's mind, and he took her by the hand and walked her back to the hunting cabin. She felt her hand shaking.

"Daisy, you have been great. Your unspoken concerns are quite a normal reaction. Each hunter goes through that dilemma after hunting his first prey. Understand that once upon a time, human beings were hunters to survive, so hunting is a normal action in life. Please let's celebrate your success now!"

Daisy was surprised by Jack's extremely polite and sensitive words. She was embarrassed when tears ran slowly over her pale cheek.

"Yes?" was all she was able to respond at this moment.

It took her a while to recover before she added, "I know. It was my own decision to become a hunter, and still I hesitate about ever hunting again."

After the prey had been carried away, all the hunters gathered in Mr. Barns's lodge near the cozy fireplace and enjoyed a glass of tasty red wine. All wineglasses were raised and a big toast given to the successful hunter. Daisy was the hero of the day. Obviously, she enjoyed every moment of her position to be the star of the day!

As the evening got under way, a catering service drove up the driveway and soon served an exquisite dinner. Jack's brother was sharing unbelievable hunting memories, and the other hunters chimed in with jokes. It was a loud and enjoyable dinner.

Daisy started to flirt with Jack Barns, who was clearly still impressed by the hunting woman.

B ack in England a week later, Daisy was happy to have a new subject to brag about at her bridge club. However, none of the other women seemed interested in Daisy's hunting experience. At first, they suggested the entire story was made up and not reality. After Daisy showed them some pictures of her kill, they were disgusted by her brutality. How could a woman shoot such a beautiful wild creature!

Daisy's efforts to impress her new girlfriends worked the opposite way. Daisy was increasingly ignored in the local women's club, and she finally decided to quit playing bridge.

However, Daisy's hunting success made her more eager to travel now and to experience other extravagant events with her husband.

21

Shortly thereafter, Jack Barns invited his friend Bernard, along with Daisy, to join him for a special social event in Paris. Daisy was thrilled to spend a weekend in Paris, and they checked in at the Hôtel de Crillon, one of the best hotels in town. She was looking forward to meeting many sophisticated personalities, and of course the presence of Jack Barns enhanced her trip.

Many important people joined that dinner party.

Daisy was wearing a sexy dark blue dress, and around her neck were four strings of expensive pink shiny pearls. She absolutely wanted to impress Jack with the fine lines of her body. She had to admit that the presence of Bernard's friend Jack was the only reason she joined the party, as she was fond of this generous and kind gentleman. She hoped to be seated next to him. However, Jack, who was clearly not aware of Daisy's intention, had her sit next to an American businessman who could not speak any French.

Mr. McCrummy was also residing at their Paris hotel. He was extremely polite, had blond hair and blue eyes, and was wearing an elegant white blazer. He seemed wealthy and reliable. Henry McCrummy was in search of new European products to import to North America. Bernard had dreamed of expanding his business to the United States for a long time, so Daisy introduced Mr. McCrummy to Bernard, who sat across the table. An interesting discussion started between the two men. Daisy's plan was to find a moment to leave her table neighbor to have a conversation with Jack. However, Jack was involved in a discussion with his table neighbor, a French businessman, and did not even take notice of Daisy's approach. Daisy did not have command of the French language, so she therefore pretended to walk toward the toilet. After a while, she returned to her seat next to Mr. McCrummy.

At this point, McCrummy was suggesting becoming Bernard's nationwide representative and distributing Bernard's products all over the States.

The next morning, Bernard signed a preliminary contract, and Mr. McCrummy invited Bernard to meet him in a week or two at his office in the outskirts of New York City.

McCrummy, sensing big money, returned immediately to the United States and started to promote Bernard's product line by contacting potential clients, promising them the impossible, and having them sign contracts for horrendous amounts of money.

McCrummy's sole interest was to make a lot of profit and be able to build a big house soon. He was not interested in checking with Bernard as to whether his promises toward the new clients would be practicable or if the short delivery deadline of the product was possible. McCrummy had no intention to serve or follow up with the new clients once he had collected their first payments.

He was a jerk, and he took any opportunity to make money and become rich. He could not care less about Bernard's serious long-term business ethics.

D aisy was eager to join Bernard on his trip to New York. She believed that in America everything was bigger, better, and more luxurious. In addition, she assumed that Mr. McCrummy was rich and would invite them to many interesting places, theaters, and good restaurants. Daisy knew that meats and fruits were much bigger and even tastier in the States. Houses had larger rooms, and the kitchens were spacious, with huge refrigerators. Daisy imagined that each house had a beautiful garden with a large swimming pool and most families own two or three cars. Her imagination was endless. She wanted to experience the American way of life and compare it with her English lifestyle.

Two weeks later, Daisy persuaded Bernard to spend first an extended weekend together in New York at an expensive hotel, attending a Broadway show, and after the weekend, visit McCrummy's business.

After their first evening in New York, Daisy got a message that her mother had been in a car accident and had suddenly died. Her father begged her to come home for the funeral. Daisy was furious over this message after she finally made it to New York.

The moment she got this sad phone call, Bernard was out buying tickets for a Broadway show. She decided not to transmit this terrible message to Bernard, as there was no way she would return to England only to attend her mother's funeral.

Since the time she had left her hometown, her relationship with her parents, the grocery store owners, was not the best. After she became such an extravagant, rich, and culturally educated city woman, Daisy saw no point in seeing her family and all the locals.

She and Bernard had made it to New York for an exciting weekend, and she would rather explore the city and later be spoiled by Mr. McCrummy, Bernard's new business partner, than return home and be reminded of the humble life of her childhood.

They went to a Broadway show and afterward had dinner at a fancy steak house. Daisy was in awe of the luxury and fine food served. She was content with what New York could offer.

Henry McCrummy's place was far off the city center. It took Bernard and Daisy more than three hours to finally find his office. It was an old shack in an industrial area.

Daisy was extremely disappointed to find herself in such a run-down area. Surprisingly, many men, including the police, surrounded the trailer office. Bernard asked one of the police officers if this was really McCrummy's office and what was going on. At first, the officer seemed reluctant to answer Bernard's question in Daisy's presence. Bernard pulled his airfare ticket from his pocket and explained to the officer that his trip overseas was a scheduled appointment to meet McCrummy today. After the officer checked Bernard's flight ticket, he began to explain the unforeseen situation.

McCrummy's employees had decided to go on strike because he did not pay them their weekly salaries for over a month. Furthermore, the workers found the office entrance door blocked that morning by a truckload of garden clippings and excavation material. The employees contacted the police. The officer continued to explain that Mr. McCrummy had a long-lasting fight with a client not delivering prepaid goods, which resulted in a complicated lawsuit. Due to the never-ending delay, this client got in such a rage that he ordered his site manager to unload a truck of tree and garden clippings right at McCrummy's front door!

Daisy, in her elegant lime-green pantsuit, and Bernard, wearing a dark blue blazer, found themselves totally displaced while surrounded by the disgusting mess. Daisy had expected a luxurious office building with large windows and many employees, with an elegant secretary at the front desk. Daisy's elegant appearance didn't look adequate. She seemed more like she was acting in a soap opera among many upset employees, the four police officers, and the arriving fire engine.

Ten minutes later, Henry McCrummy drove up his driveway in his old, banged-up, once-elegant white Mercedes. He looked extremely surprised to find the police, the fire truck, and his employees with banners reading "On strike" in front of his office.

"What is going on here!" he yelled.

"Get back to work immediately!"

Only then did he acknowledge Daisy and Bernard, and he politely said, "Oh, hello, Mr. and Mrs. While. I was not expecting you here so early this morning. Please follow me into my office."

Taken aback, he stared at the pile of material and garden clippings piled up at his front door. His head turned red, and he angrily jumped around full of rage shouting, "I will kill the devil that did this to me!"

One of the policemen took him by the arm and tried to calm him down, but with no result. McCrummy's face turned even darker red while he was swearing and kicking some garden clippings with his feet. In his rage, he totally forgot the presence of Mr. and Mrs. While.

After this incident, Bernard knew that McCrummy could

never be a serious business partner. Bernard wrote a note to Mr. McCrummy, telling him to stop all activities regarding his products and mentioning that he no longer had any intention of working with him. Bernard handed the note to one of the police officers and asked him to give the message to Mr. McCrummy.

23

Disgusted and deeply disappointed, Bernard and Daisy left the messy place and boarded their rental car, driving straight to the airport. The same day, Daisy and Bernard flew to the West Coast, where they had a meeting scheduled with another potential client in Seattle.

On the plane, Daisy ordered a gin and tonic, Bernard a whiskey. Neither could believe what they had experienced at McCrummy's place after the wonderful encounter they had with him in Paris. In Paris, Mr. McCrummy acted as a charming, well-educated, and polite businessman. Instead, Mr. McCrummy was a show-off and a phony. All that was the opposite of what Daisy expected from her first trip to the States. The visit to Mr. McCrummy's office was a real nightmare.

At the Seattle airport, Mr. Hopkins picked up Mr. and Mrs. While and drove them directly to his modern, stylishly designed offices. Mr. Hopkins, a well-educated and fine man, complimented Daisy's ensemble and her beautiful appearance. Daisy finally felt respected and at ease. The meeting with Mr. Hopkins went extremely well, and a preliminary contract was signed.

Bernard's new client invited them for dinner at a fancy

resort far from the city center, located near an artificial pond. Mr. Hopkins, who had lived for several years in England, was communicative and joked a lot. They enjoyed a delicious meal and tasted several excellent California wines. The three of them had a good time.

Instead of driving back through the woods on the narrow windy roads late at night, Mr. Hopkins suggested staying over at the resort hotel. Happy about the successful day and relaxing evening, Daisy and Bernard moved into their elegant hotel suite, and within a short time, they fell sound asleep.

At five o'clock early the next morning, the phone rang in Bernard and Daisy's hotel room. Daisy thought it might be her father again asking her to return for her mother's funeral, but soon she rejected that idea; her father could not know that they had left New York already.

Who else could it be, possibly Mr. Hopkins?

Nobody else knew in which hotel they resided that night. Sleepy Bernard finally picked up the phone.

"This is McCrummy. I'll meet you in five minutes in your hotel room, number two forty." He then hung up.

A shocked Bernard commented, "How on earth did Henry McCrummy find us at this remote resort? When did he fly out from New York to the West Coast? He must have boarded an aircraft only a few hours after we left. He really has extreme bad manners to wake us up at this early hour of the day. Is this a bad joke?"

As Daisy was about to answer, someone knocked at their hotel room door. At five fifteen in the morning, it was still dark outside. Bernard jumped into his trousers, put a T-shirt on, and opened the door; Daisy went to hide in the bathroom.

In front of Bernard stood McCrummy, wearing a dark gray suit, a blue shirt, and an elegant yellowish-gold tie. He was holding two bottles of Coke in one hand and an elegant leather folder in the other. McCrummy was just opening his mouth, probably to greet Bernard, but before McCrummy could say a word, Bernard said furiously, "This is absolute impertinence to wake us up at such an hour. Please leave us alone. Our final agreement is not signed yet, and I will never sign it. Our business relations are done and over. There will be no discussions any longer."

Bernard wanted to close the door of his room; however, McCrummy simply walked straight into Bernard's room, placed the Coca-Cola bottles on the table, and behaved as if it would be his room.

Then he started talking with a gentle voice:

"Dear Mr. While, we have to settle this right now. I am not going to lose the contract with you just because of the bad coincidence the other day. Let me first explain this coincidence to you in detail so you will understand that the strike of my people resulted from a huge misunderstanding …"

Bernard just waved his hand.

"I'm not ready to hear any of your excuses. Once I have made up my mind, I will never change it. Get out of this room as fast as you can."

McCrummy clearly did not intend to leave Bernard's room. Instead, he asked rudely, "Tell me, who did you meet in Seattle and where are you heading from here?"

Bernard was feeling bad-tempered and had no intention of talking with McCrummy. When McCrummy placed himself on a chair and opened his folder, Bernard pulled him off the chair and asked him to leave their private bedroom immediately. No way, Henry McCrummy stood next to the door like a millstone.

"This is none of your business, but we are invited to a private party in the San Francisco area. An English schoolmate of mine is celebrating his birthday."

"Okay, I will join you there," McCrummy insisted.

"See you at the airport."

"No, there is no way you can join us at this private birthday party. If you are not leaving this room within a minute, I will call the reception desk and have you arrested. You have been extremely impolite to wake us up in the middle of the night and rudely invade our room."

Bernard opened the door while holding the hotel phone in his hand. McCrummy had no choice but to leave the room.

Bernard was exhausted and extremely upset about that incident. He could not understand such disrespectful behavior.

Daisy, traumatized after waiting in their bathroom suite, suggested that Bernard notify the reception and Mr. Hopkins immediately.

It was six in the morning by then, and Bernard decided to call his new partner, Eddy Hopkins, and ask him for advice. By coincidence, Eddy had heard rumors about McCrummy's way of doing pushy business as well as his way of checking out people. Eddy came up with a solution to blur McCrummy's plan.

"Bernard, let's head to Portland in about an hour. You can take off to San Francisco from the airport there while McCrummy waits to meet up with you at the Seattle airport. I'll see you and your lovely wife with your luggage sitting in my car in the parking lot behind the hotel an hour from now. I'll go unlock my car right now. Please use the back exit of the hotel. In the meantime, I will pay the bill and then meet you at my car. We might have some breakfast on the road."

*

While checking out, Eddy observed a person, obviously Mr.

McCrummy, sitting in a far corner of the main lobby. He was clearly waiting to see Bernard.

Eddy Hopkins paid the resort bill and asked the clerk for a flight schedule out of Portland. Then he walked straight through the front door, pretending to wait for a taxi.

The moment McCrummy could no longer observe where Eddy was going, Eddy changed direction and walked around the hotel toward his car. Bernard and Daisy were already inside Eddy's car, and they drove off to Portland. During their drive, Eddy called his office on the car phone to find out more about McCrummy and his strange personality. They took their time driving and decided to stop at a small coffee shop for breakfast.

Hours later, they arrived at the Portland airport. And who did they spot at check-in?

McCrummy was waiting near the gate to board.

Bernard felt his temper raising. How could McCrummy check him out here? McCrummy was hunting Bernard!

24

Bernard had not left the resort through the main lobby, as McCrummy was expecting. After waiting for a while, McCrummy decided to find out more about the last client who just stopped at the cashier to pay his bill. McCrummy walked over to the hotel clerk and pretended to have found a coat, saying that probably a guest forgot it on a chair. The clerk mentioned that his guest had left in a hurry for Portland International Airport.

McCrummy rented a car and headed straight to Portland. He missed the plane to San Francisco by five minutes, and he decided to board the next plane. He asked the flight attendant if Mr. and Mrs. While were on the boarding list.

She said, "We have orders not to give any information concerning who boarded any plane."

McCrummy insisted:

"I missed my flight by five minutes, and I need to know if my friends are on board."

The flight attendant looked at McCrummy's ticket, checked her computer, and cleverly answered:

"Your name does not show on the passengers list of the plane that left five minutes ago, so I am unable to answer your question." She then walked away.

This time McCrummy's investigation plan did not work out.

He'd assumed that Bernard and his wife had left on an earlier flight.

After Bernard spotted McCrummy at the Portland airport check-in gate, he changed direction and returned to the main terminal. He asked for another flight to San Francisco. Bernard and Daisy decided to fly the next day instead. Bernard was relieved to have McCrummy off his shoulders.

Daisy was exhausted from this adventure and complained of feeling hunted like a deer by this man. Bernard decided to check in at an expensive hotel with a Jacuzzi to relax. Daisy had never experienced a Jacuzzi before, and she wanted Bernard to have one installed in their home when they returned to England.

The next morning, Bernard and Daisy flew to San Francisco and enjoyed their English friend's birthday party. Tommy had invited several friends as well as some old English schoolmates who happened to work in the Bay Area. They all had lots of memories and stories to share. It was great fun. Suddenly, Tommy's wife walked to their table, saying that Bernard was asked for at the front door. Someone was waiting there for him. Embarrassed, Bernard asked Tommy's wife if this was a good-looking, short man with a New York accent.

"He told me that you invited him to my husband's party. His name is Henry McCrummy. I will bring him to your table if you agree," Tommy's wife reported.

"No, for goodness' sake. Please send him away; he is chasing me wherever I go. I certainly do not want to see or meet that guy at all."

Tommy's wife walked off and returned two minutes later, saying, "He absolutely needs to talk to you in person."

Furious, Bernard went to the front door. After a rough

discussion, Bernard finally agreed to see McCrummy on his flight back to Europe, during a stopover in New York.

McCrummy had manipulated Bernard to do what he wanted.

Daisy realized how easy it was to take advantage of her husband.

Jack Barns fully impressed Daisy! She never forgot his kind words upon seeing her doubts after shooting the elegant elk. She well remembered the minute he took her hand after she went over to the dead elk and walked her back to his lodge. She admired the way the gentleman had acted, and of course she was taken by his wealth, as displayed by the luxurious hunting lodge. She was determined to charm him and make him realize that she admired him or even better: that she was a seasoned hunter and wanted to seduce him.

The next time Bernard was scheduled for an extended business trip to Germany and France, Daisy took the occasion to see Jack in secret. Bernard's trip was supposed to last two weeks.

Bernard returned one week earlier than planned. Daisy was not home upon his return.

The maid said Daisy had driven with a girlfriend to the city center of London to do some shopping and will be back in two or three days.

Bernard immediately sensed that something was wrong. It was not Daisy's habit to drive her car into town since they had employed a driver for that task. Furthermore, she would not stay more than one day downtown. Besides, shopping in London's city center was not her first choice!

Never before had she taken off with any girlfriend to drive into the city. If so, she would ask their driver or take a taxi.

Two days later, Daisy returned home without shopping bags. She looked stunned to find her husband already home.

"Do you need any help unloading the car?" Bernard asked.

"No, why? I had a meeting with an important person regarding your business," Daisy answered.

"Our maid told me that you went shopping with a girlfriend in downtown London," Bernard said, puzzled.

"That's correct. We went to London and ordered some clothing, and then we met this important man. On our way back, my girlfriend's car had a leak and the brakes did not work properly anymore, so we had to spend the night in a motel along the road until the brakes had been fixed."

Bernard realized that she was acting slightly nervous.

Was she telling him the truth? He was not ready for any discussion, and he just let it be.

However, he was not surprised when Daisy took off ten days later, pretending she was going to visit the Viking museum in Stockholm with her art class for two days.

Like a flash, Bernard remembered Daisy flirting with his Swedish friend Jack after the hunting adventure and how much she wanted to talk to him at the party in Paris.

Has she started an affair with Jack? he pondered.

Was he the important person she met in downtown London lately?

Daisy brought up excuse after excuse for traveling here or there, which seemed quite strange since she hated to travel unless she could reside in a noble hotel and stay for at least a week.

26

One day Bernard decided to follow her when she left.

Four hours after she left the house, he drove to the airport and boarded the next flight to Stockholm. In Stockholm, he checked in at a hotel near the airport and ate dinner at the hotel's restaurant. At about nine o'clock that night, he hired a taxi.

Bernard felt odd about spying on his friend or his wife.

Still, he was driven by an inner voice telling him that this was the question's answer.

Looking through the taxi's window, he saw the town of Stockholm disappear in the dark. After more than a half-hour drive, the cab left the main road and turned into a large open space followed by dense wooded areas. Then they passed one single farmhouse before continuing uphill toward the hunting lodge located at a lonely open lot in the woods.

Approaching Jack Barns's hunting lodge, Bernard asked the driver to stop at the parking space located two turns in the road below the hill where the lodge was situated. Barns's car was parked here.

Bernard asked the driver to wait for him, as he was just going to deliver something and then wanted to be driven back to

Stockholm. The lights were not turned on to display the narrow winding road leading up toward the lodge. Bernard had been here several times, and he knew his way around. He was nervous and felt like a hunter stalking his prey. One last bend, and then he would be near the hunting lodge.

The lodge was fully illuminated. He thought perhaps his friend had gone hunting with some people and then had them over for dinner. After dinner, Jack usually ordered several taxis to drive his friends back home. Hunting was rather exhausting, and lots of wine was consumed after a good catch.

Still, Bernard was driven by an inner voice to check it out.

Sneaking along the bushes surrounding the porch steps, he slowly worked his way toward the well-lit windows.

Through the branches of two bushes, he spotted Daisy lying in Mr. Barns's arms and kissing him. They were alone.

This cannot be reality! Bernard thought.

Bernard was simultaneously shocked and terribly hurt.

How could his beloved wife ever betray him with his friend?

Disgusted, he turned around and walked like a drunken man back to the parking area, telling the driver, "Please drive me back to my hotel now."

Bernard was not able to speak further. His heart seemed to bleed, and all his energy changed into an immense sadness. While driving off, he watched the landscape disappearing. Bernard felt like drowning in the darkness of the night. The drive back to the airport hotel seemed endless. After paying the driver, without waiting for his change, he walked like a somnambulant into the hotel hall and boarded the elevator to the third floor. It took him some time to find his room key in his pocket. He was totally confused. Today's discovery was a nightmare.

Back in his room, he pulled his shoes off and lay on the bed. He was deeply hurt and disappointed, and tears welled up in his eyes. There was no way to understand Daisy's dishonesty. He loved her and spoiled her with whatever she asked for. Jack was Bernard's friend. Bernard could not understand why Daisy would betray him with his friend. Bernard found no answer.

Worn out, he fell asleep still wearing his business suit.

The next morning, he took off on the earliest flight back to England.

Daisy returned two days later, and Bernard confronted her at dinnertime.

"Daisy, I assume that you had a good stay at Mr. Barns's lodge in Sweden."

Daisy, looking surprised, responded, "What do you mean? I was visiting the Viking museum in Stockholm with my art class. Then we drove with one of my classmates up north to visit her sister. She just had twin girls, and I wanted to see them."

"Okay, Daisy, do not take me around. I personally saw you being intimate at Jack's hunting lodge two nights ago. I returned by plane from Sweden yesterday."

Taken aback, Daisy got up, furiously threw her chair to the floor, and stomped out of their dining room, yelling, "I'm going to leave you! I'll marry Jack as soon as we're divorced. For your information, I have already called my lawyer about the divorce process."

Daisy packed some of her belongings and left the house early the next morning. There was nothing Bernard could do. She had made up her mind, and nothing would change her decision.

Bernard was shocked to find Daisy gone the next morning.

On the kitchen table, she had left him a letter saying that she was determined to enforce their divorce.

27

Bernard was so distressed. Eight months later, during a meeting in Italy, he felt dizzy. His client asked him if he had health problems. Bernard had to admit and accept that his wife had left him and that she had requested a divorce. From this point on, Bernard began to disintegrate and feel depressed. He also began to lose weight.

After that business meeting, Bernard headed back to his hotel.

He parked his car in the parking lot and walked toward his hotel room. Absent in his thoughts, he left his room key in the car.

He went to fetch it from his parked car.

A woman was just parking her car next to his. When she exited her car, her purse fell onto the ground. Bernard retrieved it for her.

"Thank you very much. That's so kind of you," she said, looking at him while she locked her car.

Suddenly, a big look of surprise passed over her face.

"Aren't you Bernard? Remember many, many years ago, when we went to the same school way back in England?"

Bernard was not in the mood to meet anyone at this moment, yet he moved his eyes from the purse to the woman's face.

His jaw dropped. "Graziella?"

28

Graziella was a beautiful and intelligent girl, half Italian and half English, with reddish-blonde hair and soft dark brown eyes. During high school, Bernard admired her a lot, not to mention that they were attracted to each other. Graziella was a loving person, easygoing, charming, and never demanding. Bernard was sad when Graziella's parents decided to move back to Italy. Graziella and Bernard wrote beautiful letters to each other. Graziella's family moved three more times following her father's job.

Bernard lost contact with his "old girlfriend" the day he had to join the army and go to war. Years later, when he returned home, nobody knew or could find Graziella's address; she had moved again. During their high school time, Bernard's parents did not like this friendship too much, because Graziella's mother descended from an Italian farmer's family and her father was an electrician. His parents expected Bernard to marry an aristocratic English girl.

"Bernard, what a coincidence to meet up with you here! I moved back to England after I became a widow two years ago. Now I'm going to visit my in-laws in the neighborhood of Florence for a few days."

Bernard had to pull himself back into reality.

"Graziella, this is a great surprise. I just returned from a business meeting. Would you join me for dinner at the hotel restaurant in about fifteen minutes?"

"Yes, why not? We might refresh some of our school memories and catch up on everyone's life. Bernard, are you married?" Graziella asked.

"Yes, I am—or I *was* married." After a short pause, he added, "My wife, Daisy, left me a few months ago and is divorcing me."

Both walked toward the hotel entrance. Bernard went straight to his room. He felt relieved to have shared his upcoming divorce with someone he once knew so well. Graziella was the first person to whom he'd mentioned his disturbing pain.

*

Graziella watched her dear old friend walking toward his room. He appeared to be carrying a heavy load on his shoulders. She sensed his pain.

29

After Daisy left their beautiful villa, she never returned. She found a small but elegant apartment in the outskirts of London, facing a public park. A list of furniture and things she needed from her villa had been sent by her lawyer to Bernard, with the order to have it shipped to her new apartment. The new living room had to be painted a warm yellowish color to complement her white leather sofa and yellow and dark blue pillows. Her stylish glass table was sitting on an expensive Persian rug that covered half of the wooden parquet.

Everything needed to be perfect. Her intent was to move to Sweden and marry Jack Barns as soon as possible. She dreamed of being spoiled by this rich and noble man. Daisy was ready for a new adventure, and she did everything to reach this goal quickly.

30

Daisy and Bernard's children were now attending a boarding school about eighty miles from home. To save money, Daisy had laid off their maid who'd looked after their two children year after year. Daisy was disappointed one day when she heard the children mentioning that they loved this lovely old woman even more than they loved their mother.

The children were terribly shocked and sad after reading their mother's short message sent by mail.

Dear children,

This is just a short note to let you know that I decided to leave your dad and that I demanded a divorce. I moved to a small apartment at the opposite end of town and will let you know my new address shortly. Please do not ask for a reason. It is just time for me to make a change in my life. You are almost grown up, and you do not need your mother around you any longer. Soon you will be able to look after yourselves.

Regards,

Mom

Finally, Daisy felt she was free to do whatever she wanted.

Many mutual friends could not understand Daisy's decision in leaving Bernard. So Daisy decided to break contact with her children and most of her and Bernard's mutual friends. She feared having to explain the truth to them. Her goal was to proceed with the divorce and finalize it as soon as possible.

Also, she asked Bernard for a large sum of money, and she was not fully aware that her outrageous demands automatically would turn the divorce into a long-lasting process.

31

Daisy went to visit Jack in Sweden every second weekend. Often they went hunting together alone, and sometimes they spent time with Jack's friends at his luxurious lodge.

About one year later, Jack Barns surprisingly refused to see Daisy at his hunting lodge. He unexpectedly told her that he was no longer in love with her and that he never intended to marry her.

"What's the reason?" Daisy asked, perplexed under her tears.

Calmly, Jack answered, "I discovered that you lied to me. Do not ask any additional questions. It is finished and over! Please board that car waiting outside. My driver will take you back to the airport and please never show up again. Good-bye!"

Jack opened the door of his lodge, walked her to the waiting car, literally pushed her onto the seat, and closed the door. He turned around and walked straight into his lodge without looking back. The front lights of the hunting lodge were turned off immediately, even before the car took off.

"Ma'am, I will drive you directly to the airport; the fare has been paid in advance," said the driver.

Daisy was driven by an unknown driver through the woods late at night, having no further conversation with the driver.

Daisy felt terribly hurt, and many tears ran down her cheeks.

After driving half an hour through the immense woods, her anger swelled up and Daisy started thinking of revenge.

She realized there was no way to return to what she'd had.

Why did Jack kick me out of his life?

She could not figure out any reason. He was a bachelor and seemed not to have any girlfriend. Jack let her fly to Sweden and come all the way to his hunting lodge only to brutally kick her out of his cabin today.

Possibly Jack could have talked to Bernard?

Daisy was furious, devastated, and disgusted.

After leaving the car, she decided to check in at the airport hotel without eating any dinner. In her room, she threw her bag onto her bed and went in the bathroom to splash cold water on her face. She checked her face in the mirror: she looked exhausted and worn out. She returned to the bedroom and flopped on the bed. Unable to sleep, she opened a book. However, she couldn't focus on the words. Loaded with anger she ripped her book apart page by page and decided to punish both men: Jack and Bernard.

She did not even consider that it was all her own fault.

32

Back home, she found out that Bernard had sold their luxurious villa in the meantime and had moved into a penthouse located closer to the London airport.

What next?

Daisy's anger grew enormously after this huge disappointment. She was blaming Bernard for all her misery.

Her way of revenge was to check the status of Bernard's life now. Several times she secretly followed him to the airport, checking if he was flying unaccompanied! Did he possibly have a girlfriend? Was he still working in France, Germany, and the United States? In which hotels would he reside during his trips abroad? She would even call hotels to ask if he was sharing his room with someone else. None of the information she gathered was useful in accelerating the divorce procedures.

*

After Bernard realized that Daisy was checking on him, he was totally disgusted. To stop Daisy from her prying investigations, Bernard's lawyer enforced a court order saying that Daisy had no rights to check on him and harass him any longer.

33

S ome years later, she found out that Bernard came down with
a serious illness. His health turned weak and weaker. He had
to stop working from time to time. His cancer progressed, and
he finally had to be permanently hospitalized. His cancer was
terminal.

At this point, Daisy concluded that she might be better off
as Bernard's widow rather than as a divorced woman. She would
certainly get far more money.

She absolutely had to find out how long he would live. She
needed to see him at the hospital.

*I must find out where he is hospitalized and visit him in secret. There
must be a way to go about it.*

She assumed that perhaps he might not recognize people
anymore and decided to check on him under a cover name or as
an unknown person.

It was clearly in her best interest that he die before the divorce
was finalized. Daisy envisaged helping him die, even poisoning
him, not to alleviate his pain but to achieve her goal. He *had* to
die now!

This thought drove her to plan a secret way of accelerating
Bernard's sickness and therefore influencing his death.

So she came up with the idea to buy the purple hat to hide under and visit the hospital, pretending to be an executive of the health department, checking on the nurses.

Her plan turned out to be a disaster!

34

After Daisy's dramatic visit to the hospital on Tuesday, April 7, she left the taxi so anxiously that she gave the driver a fifty-dollar bill and walked away. She then ran toward the apartment house, nearly banged her head at the entrance door, and barely made it to the second floor. It took her a while to find her apartment key in her purse because her hands were shaking. She unlocked her apartment door, and once inside, she locked the heavy door twice. Dizziness mixed with fear made her shiver.

I was on the verge of becoming a criminal, she reflected.

Half-paralyzed, she realized the immense risk she took to see Bernard in the hospital. She could have been caught carrying the poison in her purse and ended up in jail!

Still, Bernard has to die soon!

Completely exhausted but her adrenaline racing, Daisy toddled into her living room and sat down on her leather sofa. It was not even ten in the morning, yet she needed a glass of whiskey to calm down. For the moment, she was too shaky to get up.

Daisy stared at her glass table holding a vase with faded white tulips. Some flower leaves had already fallen onto her table, and yellow pollen covered a small area. Through the window, she saw a leafless birch with its white bark. It was early February and normally the landscape was enveloped by a dull gray mist. Yet today a little sun tried to penetrate the mist. Daisy was unable to appreciate the warm light as she stared through the window.

For a moment, her thoughts went back to her upcoming divorce. Then she got lost in thinking over her life with Bernard. She remembered the good and lovely years until their love had faded in a similar way to the tulips on her glass table. The loose tulip petals had lost their white color and turned an ugly yellowish gray, similar to the skin on her hands.

Daisy collected some of the tulip petals and disposed of them on the floor. She was still not able to get up and bring them over to the wastebasket. Her knees felt like jelly, and she was totally worn out.

Her thinking stopped ...

Did she fall asleep? After an hour, she made it over to the counter. With her hands still trembling, she poured a double whiskey into a clear crystal glass. She needed to sit down before drinking. Her whole world seemed to be tumbling even before consuming any alcohol. Her thoughts jumped from one issue to the next, and she questioned herself:

Why did my visit to the hospital turn out to be such a nightmare after I prepared every detail so carefully?

Why did I never envisage the possibility that someone could be in my husband's room?

Who was that woman?

Daisy did not know her at all.

Rumors had come to her ears that Bernard was dating an old girlfriend from school.

In her mind, she reviewed the time when her life with Bernard took the big change. This was after Bernard found out about her having an affair with his friend Jack Barns at the hunting lodge.

At that time, she was dreaming of great happiness by becoming

Jack's wife. She enjoyed being spoiled by this rich man. He was single, and there was no risk in meeting him in his hunting lodge every second weekend. Nobody could disturb them there. Daisy decided to divorce Bernard because she was eager to experience a new life with Jack in Sweden. She told Jack that her marriage had been a disaster for over five years, which obviously was a lie. In addition, she pretended that their divorce was already nearly finalized. Daisy had made up the whole story, and therefore she needed to accelerate her divorce.

Daisy was extremely shocked the day Jack Barns cruelly refused to see her at his hunting cabin. She did not understand his reason for brutally kicking her out after she had travelled from England to see him for the weekend.

Jack was exceptionally nervous when he told her that he was no longer in love with her. What might have changed his mind so abruptly, after Jack had admitted his love for her a month earlier?

It was incomprehensible to her that he decided not to explain his reason or to see her any longer. Jack and Bernard had been friends long before her love affair started.

Could it be that the two friends revealed the truth?

Probably Bernard called or met Jack after he discovered her love affair at the hunting lodge.

Daisy was hurt, terribly hurt. To be refused by Jack was her biggest disappointment in life.

Now sipping at her second glass of whiskey in her apartment, she realized how truly exhausted she was. Reality vanished in a cloud, and it did not take long until Daisy fell sound asleep on her white leather sofa.

Daisy woke up when her living room clock struck 3:00 p.m.

It took her a moment to get back in today's reality. The empty whiskey glass in front of her let her remember her unsuccessful visit to the hospital.

She started pondering. Bernard was definitely terribly sick. He had no chance to survive his illness. For a fraction of a minute, she felt slightly sorry for him. Daisy had to admit that the affair with Jack was a terrible mistake. After Jack had mentioned that she did not tell him the truth, she was devastated. However, Jack was a loyal man and would never cheat on his friend Bernard.

Daisy was thinking about her actual situation repeatedly:

I punished myself by being greedy and too money oriented.

There is no way to return.

How can I continue my life?

Jack is history, and Bernard is dying!

It's too late to stop the long-lasting divorce; still, I want to be Bernard's widow. How can I make that happen?

She hated Jack and Bernard, but most of all, she hated herself.

Still sitting on her sofa in front of the empty whiskey glass, her mood changed to revenge, and she decided to take new action by checking out other possibilities to achieve her goal within the next days.

Bernard has to die!

35

Daisy decided to call her daughter, Nicole, and find out if she or her brother, William, knew more specific details about the stage of their father's illness. To Daisy's disappointment, Nicole didn't answer the phone. When she dialed William's number, she was informed that the number was no longer in use. The information service told Daisy that he had moved out of town more than eight months ago.

Finally, Daisy decided to call their former nanny; she might know how to reach her children. Daisy knew that both children maintained contact with the loving old woman.

She answered the phone immediately.

"What a surprise to hear from you, Mrs. While. What can I do for you?"

"I'm sure you have the telephone numbers for my two children. I need to call them because of an emergency."

"Well, William told me over half a year ago that he is moving to Scotland but without leaving me any address or phone number up to this day. A week ago, I attended Nicole's wedding. The young couple took off on their honeymoon to Florida, and after that her husband was preparing for a move abroad. For now, they did not know if it would be the United States or Europe. That's all I know, Mrs. While."

Daisy rudely placed the receiver without saying thanks or good-bye. Both of her children had turned away from her totally.

Daisy did not even know about Nicole's marriage or who her husband was!

Her plan to find out more about Bernard's health situation had been destroyed.

"The whole world is unfair to me!" Daisy shouted aloud, full of rage.

Then she picked up her empty whiskey glass and threw it vehemently into the fireplace. The crystal broke into many pieces, and one tile over the fireplace suffered a large crack. With tears in her eyes, she stared at the many splinters of glass spread among the faded tulip leaves on the floor and in front of the fireplace. All reflected the disaster she was in!

What shall I do now?

How long might Bernard's life last?

She needed a new plan to ensure that Bernard died soon.

36

She must find a way to achieve her goal. Daisy decided to meet with a guy who was working at the nearby hospital. She had met him previous times, and by paying him some money, he had given her a hint in which hospital Bernard was transferred after his health became critical.

Now she intended to meet this guy at a remote place to plot a way to poison Bernard. For money, he certainly would help her.

When she tried to contact him, his answering machine said that he was on vacation for another week.

"Nothing is working out today!" she screamed.

Haunted by many thoughts, she was unable to sit still in her apartment. The woman sitting next to the patient's bed could have informed the police that she tried to enter Bernard's hospital room and disturb his privacy.

She decided that the solution was to take some days off and go anywhere she needed to escape from her apartment right now.

More than anything, she needed to escape from her thoughts, escape from herself.

37

Her neighbors should not see her in this stage of rage. She packed a few clothes in a small suitcase, sneaked down the stairs, and drove away. It was almost five in the evening.

Driving down the road, she was unable to decide where to go. She simply continued driving straight and eventually ended up on a narrow country road. After another half hour, she arrived at a village she had never been to before. Here she spotted a small inn and decided to stop for a stay.

For the first time in her life, she entered such a simple and undemanding place. Her room was small and had only one single window, which was facing the woods. The bed was placed in a corner. Opposite it was a chest with six drawers, a rocking chair, and a square little table with a set of playing cards on it. The material of the drapes and the bedspread had the same pattern of small blue roses. It was cozy, yet not the luxury she was used to.

After unpacking her few clothes, she went to lie down on the bed. She fell asleep immediately. At seven o'clock, the farmer's wife knocked on her door. When Daisy opened the door, the woman said kindly, "Excuse me, dear. I was just wondering if you would like to eat dinner with us in about half an hour. I need to know what you prefer."

Daisy was hungry and remembered that she had not eaten anything throughout the entire day. Surprised by this gentle person, Daisy agreed to have fish, salad, and rice.

38

Having spent ten days at the small inn, she called the hospital guy again. He was home!

She arranged to meet him on her way home.

One hour later, she was sitting at a truck stop far from her apartment, waiting for him to show up. It started pouring, and Daisy watched the leaves of the trees bending under the heavy rain. Some spring flowers near her window seat fell apart, and the wind blew the petals away. Gray clouds covered the sky totally. There was no hope of sunshine all day. Daisy shivered. After waiting more than three quarters of an hour, she started to get nervous.

Would the guy ever show up?

In her head, she was rehearsing what she wanted to say to him.

I think you are not treated too well at your job.

It's not fair to work so many hours with sick patients and earn so little money. Aren't you dreaming of a vacation in Thailand or do you have another desire?

Here she would wait and listen for his reaction and then continue.

You see, I greatly appreciated your help last time and what you did for so little money. Would you like to earn some more money?

At this moment, the awaited guy entered the restaurant.

He was tall and slim and did not convey a confident personality. He wore old faded jeans and a pink T-shirt. His curly reddish hair, his freckles, and his blue eyes gave him a look of a spoiled and insecure little boy.

After he sat down, Daisy offered him a good meal while asking how his vacation went. He answered, "Well, all was super until the last minute, when I returned my room key at the reception desk. Going back to my car, I discovered that in the meantime, my luggage had been stolen from my car, including my money and my expensive camera. I was left with only my car keys in my pocket. It was a big hazard driving back home while not knowing if the fuel would last."

This came into place with Daisy's plot.

"Well, so you are certainly in need of cash. I can offer you a well-paid assignment."

And she asked him to help poison Bernard.

By chance, the guy was scheduled for an educational exchange program, working two weeks from now at Bernard's hospital.

Daisy looked around to see if anybody was watching them. The restaurant was almost empty, except for two farmers laughing and drinking beer at the counter. Daisy handed him the poison she had prepared in an empty, small perfume bottle and asked the guy to add it to Bernard's food at an appropriate moment.

The guy who was badly in need of cash at first hesitated but then accepted the bundle of bills Daisy offered him.

After she had paid for their food, they left the small restaurant and drove off their separate ways.

39

Back at her apartment, Daisy emptied her mailbox and unpacked her small suitcase. Then she looked at the newspapers before checking her accumulated mail.

Her breath suddenly stopped, and she felt a sting in her heart. There was an obituary notice indicating that Bernard had passed away four days ago.

Bernard was dead!

Bernard was already dead?

Daisy was elated and thrilled by the "good" news.

Yes, she had bought the guy's services for nothing, but she couldn't care less.

Now being Bernard's widow, she had to attend his funeral, scheduled the next day. Immediately she went out to buy a decent black dress, a blazer, and a small black hat. Relieved, she thought, *Finally I am Bernard's widow!*

40

The next day, well dressed in her new black outfit, she left her apartment by taxi for the cemetery where Bernard's funeral was to take place at two in the afternoon. Walking through the gate with many other people and business colleagues of Bernard's, she encountered Jack. He seemed surprised to see her there. He nodded his head coldly and walked quickly over to the opposite side of the gate.

Almost at the same minute, Bernard's lawyer walked straight toward Daisy. In a distinguished but resolute voice, the lawyer told her that the judges had ruled for the divorce six days ago. The official papers should be in her mail and were delivered to her a few days ago ...

Daisy's face turned pale, and instead of being pleased that her divorce had finally been resolved, she shouted with an icy look, "I am now a widow! I don't need the divorce anymore."

While some people turned around and stared at her, the lawyer quietly told her, "Dear Mrs. While, it's too late. The divorce was finalized six days ago, so today you are not his widow but his divorced wife! By the way, it was your own choice to ask for the divorce."

These words hit her like a ton of bricks falling onto her. Daisy felt terribly humiliated in front of all the funeral guests, among them Nicole, her daughter, with her husband, and William, her son, whom she had not seen in many years.

Both of her children turned away the moment they saw her, letting her feel that she was an unknown person to them. Daisy mumbled, "Oh my God," looking down at the ground in total mortification. She was desperate and lost. When the lawyer asked her to leave the cemetery right now, she shouted, "You cannot prevent my being here! I am his widow … or was his wife."

Calmly the lawyer unfolded a legal paper and told her in front of their children and some friends that it was Bernard's last wish not to let her ever participate at his funeral.

"Mrs. While, the divorce went through before Bernard died, so there is no reason not to follow Mr. While's last will."

This was like a shotgun blast!

Bernard's lawyer grabbed her arm firmly and formally and walked Daisy out of the cemetery. He ordered a taxi, prepaid it, and sent her home.

Truly mortified and desperate, Daisy looked back hoping that someone would help her. All of a sudden, she recognized among the people gathered the woman who was sitting next to Bernard's bed some days ago.

*

Graziella observed Daisy leaving the cemetery, a scene of total social embarrassment. Graziella turned around to Bernard's graveside and thought, *His last wish has been fulfilled.*

Big tears ran down her cheeks as she placed five red roses on Bernard's casket.

95

41

Graziella's thoughts flashed back to the day when the lady with the purple hat entered Bernard's hospital room. Every single detail and even the conversation with Bernard came back to her mind.

After Daisy had left the hospital room, Bernard woke up. He asked Graziella, who was sitting next to his bed, "Was someone in my room?"

Graziella answered calmly, not wanting Bernard to be bothered.

"No, Bernard, a woman just missed the room number."

"My dear Graziella, I know I am old and sick, but tell me the truth. Was I dreaming or not? I saw a woman with a huge purple hat entering my room, and I am convinced it was Daisy."

Graziella, wanting to keep him relaxed, answered, "How do I know? I never met her. I do not believe that she would have the courage to enter this hospital since she has no authorization by your lawyers to visit you anywhere."

Bernard thought deeply for a little while and then commented nervously, "Well, first thing is that I hope to be able to survive until the divorce is final and over. It cannot be longer than another week or two. Second, I want you to know that after all that happened, she,

I mean Daisy, has no rights to ever show up at my funeral! This is my last wish. Please, Graziella, have this written down by my lawyer today. I do not want her to spill one false tear in front of my friends."

Graziella was concerned by Bernard's reaction, and she responded, "Okay, Bernard, I will call your lawyer immediately."

Graziella phoned the lawyer as Bernard went back to sleep.

She remembered that it was early afternoon by then. The air in the patient's room was sticky. Graziella opened the window just for a few minutes. Outside, only a few birds were singing; spring was on its way; nature was hiding under a thin haze.

Graziella was contemplating the beautiful surroundings. She appreciated the calm moment while Bernard inhaled the fresh clean air. She spent all night and morning near the patient. She knew that it would not last too long and Bernard would close his eyes forever. She had to face this sad moment; however, she appreciated the years they did spend together since their encounter in Florence. Their love had started in high school, and many years later, it bloomed up again.

Daisy had pretended that her divorce was already pending and she never intended to change her mind. She was in love with Jack. However, after Bernard had called his friend Jack and the truth came out that their divorce was not at all enforced at that time she dated Jack, Jack was extremely shocked, and therefore he expulsed Daisy immediately.

After a short rest, Bernard woke up again. He said, "Graziella, I know I will die soon. You know how much I appreciated your helping me after Daisy left and how much I love you for being so good to me. You have never been demanding. You are a great and giving person. You are so precious devoting hours and hours sitting next to my hospital bed."

He added after a deep breath, "Graziella, I loved you in high school. The war separated us, and we lost each other for many,

many years. When life turned sad for both of us, faith brought us back together. Isn't it beautiful that we have been able to spend some good and beautiful years together?"

Still lost in thought near Barnard's graveside, Graziella remembered that only a few days later, the court had decided upon the divorce, and it was finalized. Bernard had just awakened when his lawyer entered his hospital room with these words:

"Bernard, you made it!"

Graziella observed the great relief on Bernard's face.

Along with the official papers, the lawyer brought a bottle of red wine. Graziella asked the nurse to bring them three glasses.

Bernard, the lawyer, and Graziella celebrated the news in the hospital room. Bernard was smiling. This was the last highlight in his life. He died peacefully the next day.

*

Now Graziella had to face Bernard's funeral.

Never would she have expected Daisy to show up at the funeral, and even worse, Daisy had to be walked out of the cemetery by Bernard's lawyer.

42

Daisy was in total shock, speechless and mortified that she let it all happen. Her children, who did not even want to look at her, Anthony Bernard's friend Jack, and all the other guests at the cemetery had shared the terribly embarrassing scene. Her status, her reputation, and contacts to their mutual friends were ruined.

Her feelings switched from anger to sadness. Tears dropped from her eyes and smudged her makeup. She did not remember if she paid the taxi driver or if Bernard's lawyer paid the fare in advance. The driver let her leave the car next to her apartment entrance, and he immediately drove off without a word.

Daisy was not able to open her apartment door because her hands were shaking. The key would not fit into the keyhole. After several attempts, she finally unlocked the door. Feeling miserable, she closed the apartment door.

Daisy's whole world had fallen apart.

For a while, she was leaning against the door, and then she took off her newly bought black hat and threw it on the floor. Angrily she stepped on it. Later she'd throw it into the garbage can. She pulled off her shoes and her black dress and threw them on a pile of dirty laundry in her bathroom. Feeling terrible, Daisy sat down weeping on her living room floor. With her fingernails, she scratched holes in her black stockings. She stared at the wide, clear line of silky threads ending in a big hole; a big, black hole similar to the way her life felt today.

All threads she had pulled went totally wrong.

None of her plans were executed. All her thinking to find ways to remain Bernard's widow at the end were blown away.

Why did I destroy all the good sides of my life just to run after money, wealth, and reputation? I even lost the love of my own two children. How much did it hurt today at the cemetery to see them, as adults, turn around and walk away! Nicole, with her newlywed husband, a man I have not seen before and do not know …

William, my son, turned into a handsome young man …

Both of my children turned away and did not care a bit about their mother. Both obviously let everyone feel that they do not want to see me … They considered me an unknown person or rather as an enemy. How could I miss all the important steps in their lives in becoming adults?

It was my own fault.

Tear after tear dripped from her eyes, and she began whining hysterically. Daisy could not recall how long she was sitting on the floor crying and feeling completely empty.

43

Day after day, week after week, month after month, Daisy's awareness increased, realizing that she had no friends. No one ever called her. All of her and Bernard's friends avoided any contact with her after the embarrassing incident at the cemetery. Her own children had turned away since they went off to high school after she had started the divorce many years ago. Remembering Nicole's and William's furious looks at their father's funeral, Daisy was still deeply hurt. They clearly showed that their mother did not exist for them any longer!

Nobody cared about Daisy.

44

Daisy was devastated and completely isolated.

Time was flying by. Day after day, she sat in front of her window, staring at the landscape. Spring, summer, and fall had passed. It was winter. A thick cover of snow wrapped nature in. The trees had lost their leaves. The sky was still gray and dull, and no sunshine was seen for many weeks; no birds singing. The neighbor's balcony was abandoned, as it was far too cold to be outside; night started already in the late afternoon, and the darkness seemed endless.

Two lights illuminated the small dead end road she lived on. As the night grew, the upcoming fog seemed to bleach out the lights. Rarely would a car drive by.

Some neighbors had left for a vacation, and their shutters were firmly closed. Through the window on the house opposite, she could peek into a warm room, watching another family sitting around a table. In the middle of the table, a large red candle added to their coziness. They would play cards often. Daisy envied their pleasant and relaxed family atmosphere.

Here she was sitting all alone, lacking warmth and feeling lonely, melancholic, and bad-tempered.

Daisy became more and more depressed over her irreversible

state. She lost a lot of weight and looked extremely pale. She rarely left her apartment to go out for a walk. When she did go outside, she typically wore a long gray coat and a black scarf, with no colors or jewels at all. She did not dress nicely as she had in the past.

One day two children saw her walking along the road.

"Hey, look. Is that a ghost?" one of them said.

Daisy heard the remark and was totally shocked.

She returned to her apartment, walked straight into her bedroom, opened her closet, and checked her appearance in the large mirror. It had been months since she had looked in the mirror. Daisy met a different woman in the mirror, a person she never anticipated to be, totally different from her former elegant appearance. Her cheeks had lost their normal pink color. Her eyes had sunken into her face, showing big black circles. She had lost her smile. She had not seen a hairdresser for months. Her hair had grown wild and changed to gray. She realized that her hair would be totally gray once all the artificial color was washed out. She felt extremely old and worn out, in addition to feeling shocked at her appearance. The children in the street were right. She resembled a ghost!

In earlier times, her hair was always nicely styled; it was hazelnut colored and her face covered with smooth makeup. She was elegant and looked even younger than her real age.

Now looking into the mirror, she observed how her once elegant dress was hanging loose from her shoulders and seemed to be two sizes too large. The person in the mirror looked like a phantom. She was certain that she was going to die soon.

Disgusted, she banged the closet door hard, and the mirror burst into three pieces. She wanted to lock that terrible-looking Daisy in the closet forever. The personality she saw in the mirror should not interfere with her any longer.

Minutes later, she returned to her living room and sat down on her white leather sofa. Nothing was pleasant. Her nicely arranged apartment had turned into a mess: old newspapers were thrown on the floor, and several empty glasses were on her dirty glass table. The few flowers she had bought lately at the market had their heads hanging, as the water in the vase had evaporated.

All looked deserted and terrible.

Daisy felt totally lost and miserable.

She was lonely, and nobody cared about her.

Tears welled up in her eyes thinking about her own disaster. There was no future for Daisy.

She just wanted to die.

45

Daisy looked pale and sick and every day even worse. She felt ill and ready to enter a hospital, convinced that she would never return home. She was ready to die there.

With her last bit of energy before entering the hospital, she eliminated all her personal papers, letters, contracts, and anything that could be burned in her fireplace. She packed all her clothing, shoes, and coats in small bags, and every day she brought one or two bags to different public care associations or Goodwills. She drove two miles to a jeweler and sold all her jewelry.

One day she decided to walk down to the nearby river to dispose of her large purple hat so nobody could find it. Sitting on a bench under a tree, she watched the current. Crushing the hat between her hands and trying to tear it apart, she fractured a fingernail. Finally she threw her purple hat into the river and observed the greenish water soaking the felt material and pulling it down until it disappeared. Her self-hate was immense.

Should I jump in the river too?

She could not remember how and when she returned home.

Daisy gave her notice at her apartment for the next month's end, knowing that she would never come back. She arranged with the Salvation Army to have all her furniture removed from her apartment. Then she packed her car with only a few personal items, such as two nightgowns, some underwear, a few clothes, three pairs of shoes, a black and a gray scarf, along with her long black coat. The next day she was ready to head to the hospital, where her life would end soon.

46

About fifteen months after Bernard passed away, she told her next-door neighbor that she had become very ill and had to move into a hospital for elderly people. Obviously, nobody was interested in helping her move. Daisy had not a single friend in the neighborhood. She used to treat her neighbors quite unfairly, and she did not even greet them for the most part. Often when they walked by and gave her a friendly word, she turned her head away, pretending not to see them. She let everyone know that she did not need to talk to anyone.

Daisy needed to escape from this miserable life.

She had no choice; she was ready to die soon.

About two years later, Graziella read in a local newspaper that Daisy had passed away. There was no specific date; it simply said:

> *One year ago, Daisy While passed away in solitude.*
> *By her last will, her ashes have been blown in the*
> *wind ...*

Immediately she phoned Bernard's friend Anthony and told him about the strange note in the newspaper. Anthony had had no news from Daisy since Bernard's funeral, and he was not aware of her death. After Bernard's funeral, Anthony and Bernard's other friends broke all contact with Daisy after witnessing the embarrassing situation when Bernard's lawyer walked Daisy out of the cemetery and literally sent her home.

Anthony found out that even her children did not know where she died and when exactly. Both children had also noticed the strange note in the newspaper.

Too many questions remained open:

How, when, and where did Daisy pass away?

Why wasn't her death announced for a year?

What happened to her belongings?

She probably died alone and was thereafter cremated.

It must have been her wish to not only have her ashes blown in the wind but also have her death mentioned only after a year had passed.

It was a great tragedy, as nobody cared about Daisy.

PART 2

48

In a small village mostly inhabited by artisans and farmers, Melanie Bird lived in an old apartment house. The neighbors' back yard and some balconies limited the view. Melanie's furnished studio was small, with an old wooden bed sitting on four wooden blocks. The bed was covered with a bedspread showing bleached pink tulips. Over the bed hung a naturalistic print of a painting, framed with a heavy silver frame. It showed a bouquet of flowers in a green glass vase. Certainly the painting dated back to about 1880. In one corner of the room stood an art deco cupboard with a big oval mirror and golden art deco flowers painted on both sides. An old clock ticked on a table holding Melanie's newspapers.

This was Melanie's quiet residence.

Her days there were long, and she was lonely. Only on Sundays was there some action. Several familiar noises could typically be heard from her neighborhood. On the opposite roof, some pigeons chuckled. A dog barked, and a young mother sang a lullaby to her baby. Odors like the smell of fresh coffee mixed with a tasty Sunday meal, perhaps stew or a roast, welled up from time to time. From the neighbor's balcony, two grass parakeets imitated the young mother's melody.

A grandmother called her family to lunch. People cheered

and toasted with their wineglasses. Everybody seemed to have a good time.

A baby was crying. Dirty dishes were later piled into an old sink, and then a discussion started on who was going to take care of them. Two children started fighting. From another open window, a man with a profound voice got into a friendly conversation with his wife—a peaceful moment for both of them. From a distant road, a truck with a loudspeaker was driving by. On Sundays some farmers were selling plants and flowers out of their trucks.

Melanie watched people enjoying their tasteful lamb roast while sitting on their balcony. Happy laughing sounds came from another living room, followed by voices becoming louder and louder, manifesting the effect of the wine—they seemed to be having fun. From another floor, a baby just stopped crying. A dog slept on a narrow balcony, enjoying a small spot of sun. Dishes and plates were rinsed, and Melanie heard the rattling noise of plates, pans, forks, and spoons.

The Sunday noises increased. Two neighbors on the second floor seemed to be starting a fight. The grandmother on the third-floor balcony asked them to stop fighting. Furiously the two closed their windows.

During the midday heat, the parakeets were sleeping. Slowly the noises calmed down, the music stopped, and the discussions became less emotional. Most people retired for an early afternoon rest. For a while, the backyard turned into a peaceful area, before waking up a few hours later.

Melanie decided to rest on her bed for a while.

A telephone rang next door. After a short time, life returned. Shutters, curtains, and windows reopened, and Sunday's backyard life was reactivated. A radio speaker reported the latest sports news. The grandmother and mother on the third floor decided to take the baby out for a walk. Their dog rushed along with them. Different kinds of music sounded from two apartments. The parakeets woke up and enhanced the atmosphere with their whistling.

This was the typical Sunday family life in the South of France. Monday through Saturday, most everyone was gone working hard in the fields or on construction sites.

49

Melanie felt lonely and depressed. She wore mostly black clothing, and every day either a gray or black scarf covered her head. She wore no makeup or jewelry. Her long white hair was braided into a knot on the back of her head.

Here in the South of France she had to adapt to the special "southern" way of life. It came in handy that her mother had originated from farmers out of France and they had spoken French together during her early childhood. So Melanie was able to communicate with the locals.

*

She had sold her car in the nearby town to a craftsman who paid her cash. She saved that money in her purse and stored it later under the paper lining of the bottom drawer of her kitchen cupboard. She had her savings in cash. She did not want to open any bank account for the time being.

To return to her roots, she had to take a deep dive.

Only a few locals paid attention to Melanie, as she lived insolated day by day. One day Melanie decided to change her attitude toward people.

Her gentle landlord's wife got seriously ill, and Melanie offered to take care of her. She did the shopping daily and sometimes even cooked dinner for the landlord and his wife. Her landlord, who was a farmer, owned a small restaurant and was more than happy to accept Melanie's help. Melanie took over the task of his sick wife, selling vegetables and fruits at the farmers' market.

Soon Melanie became known as a helpful person. She was called in when a young mother was sick. Melanie took her children out for walks. Children adored Melanie.

In this remote village in the South of France, most young mothers worked, typically in the fields with their husbands or as salespeople in a department store, to help finance their lives. Most grandparents lived with their children and grandchildren in the same house. It was the grandmother's responsibility to take care of the babies and the small children until they were able to go to school. This worked out well as long the grandmother was healthy, but once the grandparents became old and sick, the young women were confronted with additional work. Often they were overloaded with their jobs and family tasks. So Melanie was called in frequently to help out. She became known as the local helper.

This village did not yet have a kindergarten. Soon the idea to start a private kindergarten and nursery crossed Melanie's mind. How to start it?

Her landlord suggested making it a village project. He placed a poster in his local restaurant, asking locals to come in after work or during any free time to help remodel his deceased parents' cottage and convert it into a kindergarten.

They painted the front door blue. Inside, a wide hall opened up to a large living room with four small windows and a glass door toward the backyard. An old-fashioned kitchen and a small dining room were next to the living room. It was a perfect setting for a kindergarten. Melanie decided to have all the walls painted light yellow. The local women were happy to sew nice curtains for the new kindergarten during their free hours after their children were asleep. Melanie's landlord was so pleased with the project that he built a playground with a swing as well as a sandbox for the toddlers. Melanie planted various flowers along the newly painted fence.

About three weeks later, Melanie's kindergarten was inaugurated. As a surprise, one of the village carpenters carved a beautiful bird and placed it near the entrance. The bird was standing on a green pole that read:

Melanie Bird's Kindergarten.

50

It did not take long before all the local toddlers attended Melanie's kindergarten. The mothers requested that Melanie continue the kindergarten even throughout the summer vacation because this was the time they had to work the fields, and they needed more help than ever.

Melanie was in her element and enjoying every single minute since the day she started her kindergarten. She'd decided to wear colorful blouses and bright T-shirts and stop covering her white hair with dark scarfs. Children loved to listen for hours to the fairy tales Melanie told them. They also loved to paint on huge white sheets of paper the newspaper printer provided at no charge. Sometimes Melanie asked children to bring one of their children's books along to share the story with the others. It was a lovely atmosphere, and all the children just adored Melanie.

They started to call her Grandma Melanie.

Every day at five, all the children went home, and thereafter Melanie cleaned up the backyard and prepared the room for the next morning. When she returned to her small furnished apartment, she was tired yet her soul was satisfied.

Her landlord had remodeled the two-bedroom flat on the top floor above the kindergarten, and he suggested Melanie move in.

He had painted the living room walls a pale lime-green and her bedroom a shade of light blue. Melanie was delighted.

Now she was able to arrange her new home the way she wanted it to be. Melanie made light blue drapes with fine white stripes for her bedroom window and placed marine-blue pillows on her bed. In the living room, she decided to have white curtains. Her new home had an elegant and fresh appeal.

From her new lodgings, she no longer needed to look onto other people's balconies. She had a lovely view over the fields and onto the kindergarten's backyard, enjoying the beautiful flowers she had planted herself.

The landlord's wife, Marguerite, had become Melanie's good friend, and she asked her to help remodel their restaurant and create the newly added rooms into cozy, appealing guestrooms after she sensed Melanie's good taste. Melanie loved to arrange rooms and choose vivid colors for the drapes and the matching bedcovers. Soon the small restaurant and the few guestrooms looked inviting for tourists to stop by and stay for a few days.

51

As the years passed, the little village became more known, and young families came to spend their vacations here. One of the big attractions was the year-round kindergarten open to the visitors' children as well.

Melanie enjoyed seeing new clients coming from other parts of France and more children attending her vacation program.

Melanie employed two additional young women to care for the many children. During summer school vacation, a new program started for first and second graders to explore the nearby woods or to visit a nearby castle. Melanie enjoyed telling them local tales.

She was happy to see some children returning with their parents the following year.

One boy told her, "My sister and I asked our parents to return to this place since we love to go on your tours, explore the area, and hear your stories while our parents ride their bikes. We never had a grandmother, and we always envied other children for having someone telling them stories or taking time for them. Grandma Melanie, my sister, and I decided that you are now our grandmother."

Melanie was extremely touched by the words of the five-year-old Giles Lagarde.

Later that day, as Melanie sat in her living room, Giles's words made her think. She never was a grandmother. Probably it was her white hair that made the boy so confident. She loved that little boy and his open way of expressing his feelings.

As the vacation went by, Giles and his two year older sister enrolled every day for the special excursions, making sure Grandma Melanie, not any other person, was guiding the tour.

One day a small group of six children went visiting an old ruin of a castle on top of a hill with Melanie. All Melanie knew was that the castle was burned down after a battle. In fact, nobody knew the original story about the owner or his enemy.

"Grandma Melanie, why don't you just make up a story, please? You are so good at that," Giles begged, and his eyes watched Melanie's lips as if the story had to drop immediately from them.

"Giles, I really don't know what to tell you, but please try to make up a story of your own and tell it to us right away."

All the children were listening as Giles shared his story:

Knight Mike entered a fight with the powerful king owning the castle nearby because they loved the same beautiful princess. The battle was brutal, and Mike's castle was set on fire. The surviving king was sure that his rival Mike had been killed in the fire and did not pay any more attention to the remaining ruin of his enemy. The powerful king was now able to marry the princess. However, in a small underground room, Mike survived, but he never went outside during the daytime. He only went hunting at night, returning before dawn. This went on for many years. One night Mike was out hunting when the king came along riding his horse. The king recognized Mike, and he was furious. "I'm going to poison you," he said.

Mike was terrified but managed to escape.

The king did not want Mike to survive, knowing that his wife, the beautiful princess, never forgot her deep love she had for Mike. The princess should never realize that Mike was still alive. The mean king employed a clever witch to find a way into Mike's hiding place and to poison him.

"Is that a possible story for that ruin?" Giles asked.

Melanie answered, "Yes, it could be, except I do not like that Knight Mike was poisoned by a witch. I think you should find a better end to your story."

Not keen about the idea of poisoning someone, Melanie wanted to change the subject, so she said to Giles while walking back to the village, "Giles, tell me where you live. What's the name of the town? You told me it's in the North of France. Is your town situated near the sea?"

52

Giles explained that they lived in Le Havre, near the Atlantic Ocean and at the entrance of the channel, in a nice home with a large garden. His father worked as a captain on a big ocean cruise ship, and his mother taught French and English at a high school. He and his sister loved their parents, and every time his dad was home, they would all do something together.

Often they were allowed to bring other children home, and then their dad would show them the cruise ship harbor with the huge steamers crossing the ocean. Sometimes his father would take them inside one of those elegant cruise ships and show his schoolmates the commanding bridge. His sister would rather be playing with her girlfriends in their garden. His mom taught the girls how to bake a cake and how to make clothing for their dolls. During vacation, the family loved to go to remote places where Dad and Mom could bike for hours. He and his sister, Bernadette, did not like biking.

Last year his dad discovered this small village here in the South of France, where everyone was happy. Plus, he and his sister could participate in the village children's program while the parents rode their bikes through the beautiful landscape.

"See, we never had a grandmother to visit or spend vacations with." At this point, Giles slipped his hand into Melanie's hand.

Melanie was touched.

Giles and Bernadette's vacation ended soon.

On their last vacation day, their father the captain came to pick up his children, bringing Melanie a beautiful green and blue silk scarf.

"We're leaving tomorrow. Our children are so happy with your program and told us that you are their vacation grandma. Please accept this small present to thank you for taking such good care of our children."

During this summer vacation, Melanie had been too busy with her kindergarten and the children's program that she had no time to help out at the restaurant, which she normally did on Saturday and Sunday evenings.

As she was walking home one Saturday and passing the farmers' market, the landlord's wife, Marguerite, called to her, "Dear Melanie, would you please take over the selling of my vegetables and fruits and help out in the restaurant tonight? I'm feeling terribly sick."

She explained that she had been standing too long at the farmers' market, and now she was ready to drop into bed with her high fever. Melanie was glad to help.

A group of five Italian bikers stopped at the farmers' market to buy some fruit. A woman who spoke a little French selected some oranges from a basket. She asked Melanie if there was a place to spend the night in the village, as their day tour was long. Melanie advised the group to ask if there were still rooms available at the only guesthouse, which was just opposite to the market. Knowing that nobody in the group was fluent in French, Melanie showed them the place.

Melanie knew that her help would be seriously needed at the restaurant since these guests had arrived and requested food.

During vacation time, the restaurant was mostly full, with all the tables taken.

The bikers were glad to find some rooms to rent as well. They liked the small guesthouse and decided to remain in the village for the next two days and rest. After the bikers brought their luggage to their quarters, they gathered around the only available round table in the guesthouse dining area. The plates were placed directly on the wooden table with white, folded paper napkins and wineglasses. Hungry as they were, they waited for the dinner to be served soon. Melanie brought a tray with five fresh salads nicely arranged on white china plates.

One of the two Italian men in the group mentioned, "We are taking a break tomorrow, so we should enjoy some of the local French red wine."

The landlord arrived personally with a pitcher of wine and freshly baked baguettes. After pouring the wine into the glasses, he said, "A la votre et bon appétit."

Switching the conversation to fairly good Italian, he said, "Melanie is a good cook. She'll broil you some steaks and serve them with potatoes and fresh beans. I hope this suits you. We do not have a big selection on our menu."

Everyone was happy with his suggestion. The bikers hungrily gobbled their salads. Melanie was asked to serve dessert to another table in the corner of the restaurant.

Bernadette interrupted her brother Giles's story about the knight Mike. "Oh, Mom, this is Grandma Melanie."

"Yeah, this is a surprise to see you here," Giles chimed in.

Melanie greeted them. "Oh! Hello, what a nice surprise. Glad to see you all here. I'm helping out tonight, as the landlord's wife dropped in bed with a high fever about an hour ago. Thank you so much for the beautiful scarf your husband brought me today; this is extremely nice of you. I will introduce myself as the so-called Grandma Melanie. All of the children have called me that since I started my kindergarten."

"We are delighted by how much inspiration you gave our children," the children's mother commented with a warm voice.

"They absolutely want to return next year, and we already booked our rooms for next July. We hope they will not be too old to participate in your vacation program."

"I do not remember if we introduced ourselves properly. I am Jacques Lagarde, and this is my wife. We are from Le Havre. Bernadette and Giles you already know."

Mr. Lagarde politely added, "When you are finished helping out, would you spare a minute and sit at our table and drink a glass of wine with us? Our children talk every day about how nice you are. There is no rush. We will sit here for at least one more hour and play cards with our children."

Melanie thanked them and mentioned that she now had to serve dinner to the Italians, saying that she might find a minute later.

After cleaning up the tables, even though Melanie felt tired, she decided to spend a few minutes with the charming Lagarde family. They'd just finished playing cards, and Giles was proud to communicate that his mother had won. They talked about their vacations and how much they enjoyed the endless bike tours they were able to take, knowing that their children are being taken care of so wonderfully by "Grandma Melanie."

Before discovering this village, they never took off without their children. Even at home, they spent most of their free time together. Jacques's parents had died when their children were only one and three years old. Mrs. Lagarde mentioned that she never had a real relationship with her own parents and that they both died before she got married. Therefore, their children had been sad not to have grandparents like most of their other schoolmates, but now Melanie had filled in this missing part. Laughing, Mrs. Lagarde mentioned that before leaving for the year's vacations both children told their schoolmates that they were going to have a good time on their vacation with "Grandma Melanie."

Melanie was touched by this open discussion and wished them a good trip back home, telling them that she was looking forward to seeing them back the next year.

Melanie was exhausted after this busy day.

When she reached her home, she sat down in her cozy living room, drinking a cup of coffee and listening to a pan flute concert. She was thinking about the happy Lagarde family. A family life Melanie had missed all these years, and now she was sixty-five years old and alone. She would have loved to have grandchildren of her own and some family bonds. However, it was too late. Melanie Bird was a lonely person without any family left, even though her life had become enriched after she'd created Melanie's Kindergarten.

Melanie was happy to know that the charming Lagarde family would come back next year and again spend their vacation in the little French village.

Painfully her thoughts flashed back to England, at the time when frustrated Daisy wanted to die and jump into the river. It was at that point that Daisy recognized her greed and all her faults. She was ready to change her life, yet to give up her life and die was not her real intention.

One gray day, Daisy took a long walk along the river near her apartment house. She knew that just after midday, there would probably be only a few people on that narrow path. Normally one or two persons were walking their dogs early in the mornings there. Therefore, she didn't expect to encounter anyone on this foggy early afternoon. She was not ready to meet anyone after she had been sitting in her living room all morning crying over her solitude. Her eyes and her face were swollen. She needed to get outside and catch some fresh air.

It did her a lot of good to be out in nature, even on a foggy day not favorable for walking along the water. As she assumed, the path was deserted. Some startled ducks shot out from the high grass, and a swan paddled away from its nest. A squirrel was running up a tree to munch some nuts in a quiet spot. For many years, she had not registered a single sound of nature. Today she felt each little pebble under her shoes, and she could even hear the sound of her own steps on the rough ground.

As a child, she often strolled along such small paths searching for frogs or peeking into a swan nest to check on its eggs. At that time, she enjoyed being alone to discover new bird nests or catch sight of some little ducklings following their mother into the water.

It had been many years since Daisy had thought back to her happy and down-to-earth childhood.

She was escaping reality and in search of a solution to change her miserable life that she had created.

After about a one-hour walk, she arrived near a virtually deserted graveyard, with no village or houses nearby. She decided to take a look at the place. Slowly she pushed the heavy, forged iron door open and entered. Nobody was around. Most graves looked deserted; possibly today's generation could not even remember the persons who died and were buried there long ago. Daisy strolled slowly up and down the narrow aisles where wild grass had grown over most of the gravel.

Some gravestones were covered with small, mossy green patches, giving the gravestones a special beauty and touch of age. Other gravestones carried bronze letters, yet the golden shine was gone and the letters looked black and dull.

What was Daisy doing here, in a place she had never visited before? For about half an hour, Daisy studied the engraved names, yet none of them seemed familiar. Still, the search fascinated her, and she continued reading more names and dates of birth and death. She concluded that the last burials happened forty years ago. There was not even one single recent grave. Suddenly, one special gravestone attracted her attention. It read:

Melanie Bird
Born 11-28-1928
Died 6-10-1947

Daisy was born on November 28, 1928.

Melanie Bird was born the same day as she was.

Melanie Bird was only nineteen years old when she died, and this was more than forty years ago. Most villagers might not even remember Melanie Bird. Daisy discovered one single faded yellow rose placed under Melanie's name. This was the only flower that had been placed in that cemetery recently. So there must be somebody who still cared about Melanie Bird's grave.

Daisy decided to walk up to the only farmhouse in sight and enquire about this deserted graveyard. The farm consisted of two houses and a stable. With a weak bark, an old black dog walked quietly toward Daisy as if to advise against her coming.

Soon an old woman wearing a dark blue apron with little white dots walked out of the stable. She looked puzzled to see a stranger walking toward her farm. She greeted Daisy politely. "Hello. Is there anything I can do for you? Rarely does a person show up out here."

Daisy was surprised by the old woman's friendliness.

"It seems I missed my trail, and then I paid a visit to the nearby deserted cemetery," Daisy answered.

"Oh, this cemetery was abandoned about forty years ago since the village decided to build a new graveyard situated much closer to the church and most of the houses. It's about a mile farther down."

The woman seemed pleased to come across someone to talk to, and she continued babbling.

"Many of the old families have died and their descendents moved away, so hardly anyone visits this place any longer. I'm about the only one going to that cemetery occasionally to bring a flower or two to the grave of my daughter. She died heartbroken two years after she got the terrible news that her fiancé had been killed in World War II. At that time, I had already lost my husband through a terrible accident. Melanie was my only child. After Melanie's death, my life became so isolated out here. Now I'm getting old, yet I am still happy looking after my flowers, my two goats, and some chickens. My only friend is my old dog. The day God decides to take me to him, nobody will care about Melanie's grave. My grave will be at the new graveyard near the village. I have no family left."

Listening to this old woman's talk, Daisy was surprised by her positive attitude after having such a hard farmer's life. This kind woman with her beautiful, clear blue eyes gave Daisy a great confidence.

"Let me make some tea for the two of us—you seem so fragile and miserable. I sincerely enjoy seeing a person out here. To be honest, you remind me a lot of my daughter."

After taking a deep breath, she continued.

"I think you should eat something and gain some weight. You look as if you are recovering from a severe illness. I have some homemade cookies; let me get them."

This unexpected kindness let Daisy forget all her grief and revenge. It had been a long time since she had a conversation with someone so kind, and she answered, "Thank you so much. I'd like to accept your offer, and I certainly appreciate your thoughtfulness."

The old woman disappeared into the house, and after a moment, she asked Daisy to come inside and take a seat at her kitchen table.

Then she asked, "And what brought you out here?"

As they enjoyed the warm tea, Daisy started to open up.

"I was walking along the river feeling totally frustrated and fed up with my own life, and now you have brightened my day."

Daisy was surprised by her own words. Still, she did not think she was up to a conversation.

The older woman seemed to sense it, and she continued to speak.

Daisy did not understand what made her feel so confident near this warmhearted woman, and she loved to listen to her talking. The old woman appeared equally delighted to see Daisy changing from a depressed person to an interested listener.

For a long time, the two sat at the bare wooden kitchen table, drinking tea and eating delicious cookies. The old woman told her that her husband fell from a cherry tree and died shortly before her daughter Melanie was fifteen years old. She and Melanie continued to take care of the farm with two employees. Melanie's fiancé was a charming young man a few years older than she was, and he was ready to take over the farm one day. However, the war totally changed their lives; after Melanie lost her fiancé on the battlefield, she refused to eat properly and died two years later. The old woman had no choice but to take care of the farm all by herself.

She originally was a trained nurse, and she had worked with the local doctor in earlier times. After she got married to a farmer, the doctor occasionally sent one or two patients out there to recover under her guidance for several days, sometimes weeks.

"I loved to still be able to take care of his patients and help them to recover. I loved my profession as a nurse. Yet this task ended after the doctor retired." The older woman grew quiet.

Daisy slowly relaxed as she sat in the warm kitchen and listened to the nice old woman speak.

Daisy got her to resume her talking by asking, "Is the picture over there of your daughter, Melanie?"

The woman stood up and brought the picture to look at it closely. "Melanie was a beautiful and happy girl, easygoing and always pleased to do whatever one asked her to do. She never complained. Everybody just adored her."

She went on to tell her that Melanie was a good student and was learning to be a children's nurse. She played the piano and sometimes asked to go to the village to play the organ in the church. When Melanie died, the only thing she left was a chest with poems she wrote to her fiancé. Beautiful poems, the woman continued.

"Would you like to read one or two? I love to talk about Melanie. Do you mind?"

"No, not at all. Please show me whatever you like from Melanie. I'd love to hear more about your daughter."

Daisy was immersed in hearing about Melanie's personality.

The old woman walked slowly up the narrow staircase to the first floor, returning with a painted wooden box decorated with ten yellow roses. She opened the box and showed Daisy several pictures of Melanie as a child, pictures of Melanie at high school, and pictures of Melanie with her fiancé. Then she opened a small high school notebook with one of Melanie's poems and handed it to Daisy.

"Please read it aloud. This would please me, as my eyes are getting weaker and I do not see every word properly any longer."

Daisy was happy observing the old woman enjoying every minute, and she started reading a poem and then a second one.

Then the old woman pulled from the wooden box two handkerchiefs with embroidery, which Melanie had made. She handed one to Daisy and said, "This one I'd like to give you as a present to remember my Melanie. You have been such a good listener, and you put so much heart into reading Melanie's poems. I truly enjoy your visit. I am so lonely out here. Would you come back and visit me again?"

It was five o'clock by then, and Daisy realized that she had to walk back all the way along the river before it started getting dark.

"Yes, I certainly would like to stop by again. Thank you so much for the beautiful handkerchief. I do appreciate it a lot. I as well enjoyed spending time with you. I'm a lonely person myself. I have to admit that it's been many years since I felt as cozy and happy as I do in your presence."

The old woman tapped Daisy on her shoulder and said, "Yes, as a former nurse, I guessed that you miss some warmth, and I am glad to hear that you feel better now."

Daisy was at a loss for words. Finally, she stood up and said, "Madam, you are wonderful. I cannot thank you enough for your gentleness. Spending this afternoon with you brought me back to my own childhood. It was a happy one ... with a loving mother. Would you mind lending me Melanie's notebook with the poems so I can read them all after I reach home? I sincerely promise to stop by tomorrow afternoon at the same time and return them to you."

"Yes. Please tell me your name."

"Daisy. Daisy While."

"Sure, Daisy. I do trust you. Please do not delay; bring them back tomorrow. They are all I have left from my dear daughter."

Daisy shook hands with the lovely old woman and walked along the river back home. On the road, she realized how much love this fine person was able to give. It was already night when Daisy reached her apartment finally. Daisy felt happy and totally changed.

Melanie's mother was an admirable woman. The simple farmer's wife had a great heart and was so positive, even after a hard life with lots of losses.

After Daisy had eaten a bowl of vegetable soup, she sat down on her sofa and read Melanie's touching poems. Once finished, she closed the notebook and thought about Melanie's touching poems. Suddenly, she found Melanie's identity card clipped on the back cover of the old high school notebook.

A previous thought popped up in Daisy's mind:

Melanie Bird has exactly the same birth date as me!

The next morning, Daisy immediately went out to copy the identity card and clip it into Melanie's booklet. Then, as promised, Daisy walked all the way back to the farmhouse to return Melanie's poems to her mother.

Melanie's mother was happy to see Daisy back with the precious notebook. Again the two women spent more than three hours talking.

This time Daisy inquired more about Melanie's life, exactly what the old woman enjoyed sharing.

This was the day Daisy decided to slip into another identity.

All of Daisy While's past had to fade away.

Daisy had to die.

The solution was to create a new future far from England and escape to the South of France, starting a new life there as Melanie Bird.

The beginning of July, Melanie was expecting the two children to come back for their vacation. At the guesthouse, she had prepared their bedroom, placing a chocolate ladybird on each of their pillows and hiding a little storybook for Giles and Bernadette under their covers.

Again the children were happy to be back and to participate in Melanie's special summer program while their parents took off for beautiful daily bike tours. Melanie took the children walking through the woods looking for special flowers, and sometimes they found mushrooms or berries.

One day they went playing near the ruins of the castle. Giles wanted to tell his invented story of why the castle was on fire after the fight between the king and the Knight Mike. However, this time the end of the story was different. Giles knew that Grandma Melanie did not appreciate his former ending at all, where Knight Mike should have been poisoned.

This time Giles proudly pretended that the king decided to transfer Knight Mike to another continent, far away from his castle. Giles then asked, "Grandma Melanie, do you like this ending better?"

"Yes, this is a perfect ending. I certainly like it much better," Melanie answered, smiling.

That evening, when Giles and Bernadette's father arrived to pick up his children, he was concerned. His wife's bike had hit a stone, and she had fallen off the bike. She had to be transported to the hospital in the next town.

When Mr. Lagarde left the hospital, she was still in a coma; however, the doctors were confident that it might not be too serious. She had broken her left arm and suffered a wound to her forehead; she also needed some stitches and seemed to be fighting a fever.

Mr. Lagarde asked Melanie if she could take care of his two children after dinner and put them to bed. The doctors had asked him to return to the nearby hospital to check on his wife. Possibly she would be out of her coma by then.

"Surely, Mr. Lagarde. Please don't worry. I will look after your children. The most important thing is that your wife will hopefully recover soon."

When the children went to bed, they loved Melanie sitting on Giles's bed and reading them a nice long story until they both fell sound asleep.

Later Melanie waited downstairs until Mr. Lagarde returned from the hospital with the good news that his wife woke up.

The doctors wanted to keep her in the hospital until her fever dropped.

Two days later, Melanie accompanied Mr. Lagarde and the children to visit their mom at the hospital. Mrs. Lagarde was already sitting up in her bed and feeling much better. Her long blonde hair was covering a small injury on her forehead, and her left arm was in a cast. Her fever had dropped, but still the doctor requested that she remain in the hospital for a few more days, until he was completely assured that no other hidden injuries could be diagnosed.

Mrs. Lagarde was happy to see her children as well as Melanie. The children reported that during their latest excursion they had taken through the woods, they had collected some beautiful stones to bring their mother. Everybody was more than happy to see Mrs. Lagarde recover soon from her bike accident. She still looked fragile but was joking and laughing with her kids.

Melanie was concerned that the visit might be too tiring, and she walked over to look at the chart fixed at the end of the patient's bed. Her intention was to make sure that Mrs. Lagarde no longer had a fever.

For a moment, Melanie's blood seemed to stop flowing in her veins. Her face turned pale. She had to hold on tightly to the bed rail in order not to faint. She slid, and her purse dropped. All her belongings scattered over the floor and under Mrs. Lagarde's bed.

Immediately, Mr. Lagarde ran toward Melanie to help her up. However, Melanie composed herself quickly and was already collecting her belongings and bending over to gather her keys, which had slid under the patient's bed.

The hospital chart read:

"Mrs. Nicole While-Lagarde, residing in Le Havre."

Nicole!

Nicole Lagarde-While, the patient, was Daisy's lost daughter. Giles and Bernadette were Daisy's real grandchildren!

Clearly concerned, Mr. Lagarde asked, "Mrs. Bird, are you all right? You suddenly got so pale. Shall I call a doctor?"

"No, no, thank you, Mr. Lagarde."

Melanie felt terribly embarrassed.

"After I slid and fell, my purse got hooked on the bed rail. My left knee hurts a bit, but I feel fine otherwise."

59

On their way home, Melanie Bird decided that her secret could never be revealed. She no longer considered herself Daisy.

In fact, to her, Daisy truly had died.

As Melanie, she had found her own daughter, a lovely son-in-law, and even two sweet grandchildren.

*

That evening after returning from the hospital visit, Melanie was exhausted. She sat in her backyard and was unable to eat a bite of her dinner.

While she was weeping bitter and, at the same moment, happy tears, a white pigeon flew near her feet and pecked at the bread crumbs that had fallen onto the grass.

ABOUT THE AUTHOR

Otilia Greco, born in the Swiss Alps, was educated in Switzerland, England, and Paris, and she is fluent in six languages. She graduated from Zurich University of the Arts (ZHdK) and developed appreciation for history and cultures.

Otilia and her husband worked internationally, lived several years in California, and reside in Switzerland now.

ACKNOWLEDGMENTS

This book could not have been realized without the support and encouragement of many of my good friends and my family. Nothing would have been achieved without the endless support of my husband, who, with love and patience, reassured me when I felt doubt and continued to support me.

A heartfelt thank-you is owed to Victor A. Schiro, my mentor, teacher, editor, and friend, for his continuous encouragement and insight into people's ways of dealing with life.

Thanks to my coordinator, editor, and publisher at iUniverse for their great support.

CPSIA information can be obtained
at www.ICGtesting.com
Printed in the USA
LVOW11s0012221217
560521LV00001B/54/P